Shani Petroff

Finding Mr. Better-Than-You

Swoon READS

NEW YORK

A SWOON READS BOOK

An imprint of Feiwel and Friends and Macmillan Publishing Group, LLC
120 Broadway, New York, NY 10271

Our books may be purchased in bulk for promotional, educational, or business use.
Please contact your local bookseller or the Macmillan Corporate and Premium Sales
Department at (800) 221-7945 ext. 5442 or by email at
MacmillanSpecialMarkets@macmillan.com.

Library of Congress Cataloging-in-Publication Data
Names: Petroff, Shani, author.
Title: Finding Mr. Better-Than-You / Shani Petroff.
Description: First edition. | New York : Swoon Reads, 2020. | Summary: After
being dumped by her boyfriend, Cam's best friends help her seek the
perfect senior year boyfriend, but she discovers that some things are more
important than boys.
Identifiers: LCCN 2019018602 | ISBN 978-1-250-29432-6 (hardcover)
Subjects: | CYAC: Best friends—Fiction. | Friendship—Fiction. | Dating
(Social customs)—Fiction. | High schools—Fiction. | Schools—Fiction.
Classification: LCC PZ7.P44713 Fin 2020 | DDC [Fic]—dc23
LC record available at https://lccn.loc.gov/2019018602

Book design by Liz Dresner

Emoji designed by Freepik from Flaticon

First Edition, 2020

10 9 8 7 6 5 4 3 2 1

swoonreads.co

For my friends—thank you for being you.

Chapter 1

"That is not art," my boyfriend, Marc Gerber, said, pointing his paintbrush at my easel.

"You are just jealous," I told him, studying my masterpiece, which admittedly looked like a big red splotch on a canvas. "People will be fighting over this one day."

"Yeah," our friend and Marc's soccer buddy Todd Slocum said, leaning over to get a better look, "to get it out of their sight."

Marc laughed. "Right? *You* take it. No, *you* take it. No, *you* take it," he said, pretending to be two people arguing over my work.

"You know . . ." I dipped my brush into the red paint. "I think your painting may need a little sprucing up."

I took a step toward him, wiggling my paintbrush at his project.

"You wouldn't." Marc's eyes had a glint to them, almost daring me to go on.

"Wouldn't I?"

I inched closer. Marc's piece was of a soccer goalie leaping for the ball to stop the other team from scoring. My boyfriend lived for soccer. "I think some red could spice it up."

"Cam . . . ," he said, unsure of what I was going to do next.

"Yes, Marc?"

I twirled the brush as if I was about to make my move.

Before I could, he wrapped his arms around me, nuzzling his head into my neck. He knew I was super ticklish there.

I squealed as I tried to pull away, accidentally painting the side of his cheek.

"Marc, Cam, stop it," our art teacher, Ms. Winters, called out. "Do not make me speak to you again."

"Sorry." I tried to look remorseful despite the fact that my boyfriend had a gob of red paint dripping down his face. I hoped I at least got some points for containing my laughter.

"Me too," Marc said.

Ms. Winters let out a sigh and handed him a cloth to wipe off the paint. Then she turned her attention to me.

"Didn't you say you had a guidance counselor's appointment this period? Why don't you just go now?"

I still had time, but I wasn't going to push it. She wanted me gone.

I was not exactly my art teacher's favorite student. Yesterday alone, she'd snapped at me eight times to stop talking and focus on my painting. It was only the first week of school, but Ms. Winters was already all business, determined to keep the class on track. And apparently, I wasn't making that easy.

I started cleaning up my station.

"What'd you do?" Todd asked me.

"Huh?"

"To get called to guidance."

I shook my head. "No idea."

Marc still had a tiny bit of paint on his face. He looked so cute, but I decided to be a good girlfriend and help him out anyway. I wiped the smudge away with my thumb, and, after checking to make sure that Ms. Winters was facing the other direction, I gave him a light peck on the lips.

Todd rolled his eyes at me. "I bet that has something to do with it. They probably figured out you lied to get in this class just to be with Marc."

I hadn't lied. Not exactly. Okay, I had. But it was for a good reason. I was not going my whole senior year without a class with my boyfriend.

"You don't think that's it, do you?" I asked.

Todd shrugged, but it wasn't his answer I was looking for. I wanted to know what Marc thought.

As if reading my mind, Marc squeezed my hand. "Relax, it's probably nothing."

I hoped he was right, but that word *probably* dug at me as I sat in the guidance counselor's office.

Why did Todd have to get in my head? I hadn't been nervous at all until he opened his mouth. But now I was semipetrified. I'd never been called to the office before—not guidance's, not the principal's, not even the nurse's.

I couldn't get in trouble: It was my senior year, and my transcript couldn't afford it. It needed to stay perfect if I had any chance of getting into Columbia, and I *really* needed to get in.

I stared at the clock on the wall. I'd been waiting to see my guidance counselor, Ms. Vail, for twenty minutes. Much longer and last period would be over.

Finally her office door opened.

"Thanks again," a tall, blondish girl said, walking out alongside Ms. Vail.

"No problem, Lissi."

My ears perked up. This was the infamous Lissi Crandall? I craned my neck to get a better look. *Everyone* was talking about her. Not that I could blame them. It wasn't every day Brooksvale High got a new student, let alone at the start of senior year. Lissi was practically a celebrity in our little Connecticut town. She'd started attending the school's volleyball practices this summer, and from what I'd heard, she'd made quite the impression. Loved by some, hated by others—this latter group included one of my BFFs, Grace Kim.

"I'll keep you posted," Ms. Vail told her, then turned her attention toward me. "Camryn Roth?"

The sound of my name made Lissi's face snap in my direction. Her eyebrows rose and her blue eyes widened. Did she know who *I* was?

We didn't have any classes together, but I guess it was possible she'd heard about me. We did have people in common. I hung out with the soccer guys, and they were all about Lissi. *She's so hot; she's so funny; she's so perfect.* I gave them more than my fair share of eye rolls over it, but I could sort of see what they saw in her. Lissi had that whole *I can command a room without saying a word* vibe.

"You can come with me," Ms. Vail instructed.

I followed her into the office, thoughts of the new girl quickly evaporating. I had much bigger things to think about.

"Have a seat," Ms. Vail said, shuffling through some files on her desk until she found the one that read CAMRYN ROTH. "Sorry for the delay; the last meeting went longer than expected."

"That's okay."

Then I waited as she flipped through my transcript. She frowned as she turned to one of the pages. I was pretty sure she even shook her head slightly, but that could have been my imagination. My right knee started shaking, moving up and down at a rapid pace. It had a mind of its own. I pressed my hands down to stop it, but it wasn't doing any good.

Ms. Vail still hadn't said anything.

"I really, really appreciate you switching me to that art class," I sputtered, trying to get ahead of the situation. "Sorry for all the emails and voice mails about it this summer. But I think it will definitely help my college applications. Can't get enough culture, I always say." I didn't always say that. I'd *never* said that. Well, except when I was trying to convince my counselor of something.

In the case of this past summer, it was getting Ms. Vail to move me into my boyfriend's class—although I never mentioned the boy-friend part to her. I may or may not have bugged her about four dozen times to get switched into Ms. Winters' last-period art class.

After the first dozen correspondences, she wrote me back with "good" news. She had managed to move me to Mr. Tobin's second-period art class. But good to her was sucktastic to me. I'd been trying to get into *Marc's* class so I could be near *him*, not to learn about pointillism and other things that made my head spin. So I doubled down, saying that the only reason I wanted to take art was to work under Ms. Winters' esteemed tutelage. Yes, I laid it on thick, and often, but I had an agenda: taking at least *one* class with my boyfriend.

I couldn't only see Marc at lunch. That wasn't happening. So I did what I had to do.

I mean, it wasn't like I gave up physics for him. I scrapped a persuasive-speaking class, which clearly I didn't need, since I was able to convince Ms. Vail to rearrange my schedule. Or so I thought. Sitting in the office had me wondering if maybe the class would have sharpened my skills.

Ms. Vail must have found out the true motive for my request.

Ms. Winters probably tipped her off. I was going to be in trouble. A detention or—worse—switched out of Marc's class. They'd probably want to make a point that what I did wasn't acceptable. I couldn't imagine the school looking too favorably on changing a student's schedule due to their relationship status.

"What? Oh." Ms. Vail waved her hand at me. "That wasn't a problem."

I sat up straighter. If that wasn't the issue, what was?

She turned a piece of paper toward me. "I actually wanted to talk to you about your college applications."

I let out a sigh of relief. *That's it?* I'd worried over nothing.

"I'm all set with that. I already started."

Now it was Ms. Vail's turn to let out a breath. "Camryn—"

"Cam," I corrected her. Unless I was getting grounded, no one ever called me Camryn.

"Cam," she continued. "You remember the assembly last year?"

I nodded. The juniors had been called into the auditorium for a lecture about life after high school, what to look for in a college, and so on. It was pretty boring, but it got me out of precalc, so I was all about it.

The guidance counselors made us fill out a questionnaire and encouraged us to set up an appointment to talk about options. The only person I knew who had actually signed up was Grace. I guess now that it was the start of senior year, they were circling back to all of us no-shows.

She pointed at the paper in front of me. "That's the form you turned in."

Scanning the questions, I couldn't help but smile. I definitely remembered filling it out. The whole college section had hearts drawn around it. I traced one with my finger.

"I've been going over everyone's files, and your answers concern me," Ms. Vail said.

I knew it wasn't so much my answers, plural, as my answer, singular. The questions read:

What is your dream school?

What is your reach school?

What is your match school?

What is your safety school?

I wrote Columbia for all of them.

"I wasn't ignoring the assignment. I just know what I want."

Ms. Vail folded her hands together and leaned forward. "Camr—Cam," she said, softening her voice, "it's good to have a reach. I just think you need to keep your options open. Columbia University is extremely competitive. I've gone over your transcript, and I'm worried you may be setting yourself up for disappointment. It's important to have backups."

I wasn't *only* going to apply to Columbia (my parents had vetoed that idea), but it was the only place I wanted to go. It was part of the plan.

"My grades are good. I got all As last year, my SATs are way above average, and I'm writing a kickass essay." I slapped my hand over my mouth. Could you say *kickass* to your guidance counselor?

"Your grades are good, but you're not in AP classes," she said, unfazed by my language, "and your SAT scores are impressive, but they'll be comparable to most of the people who apply there. You need something that makes you stand out, and your lack of extracurriculars has me concerned." She glanced back down at my file. "There's nothing here since freshman year. Not one club, team, or activity. Schools look at things like that."

"I have stuff."

She waited for me to continue.

I twisted my charm bracelet around my wrist. "I did volleyball part of my freshman year. And I would have done some clubs, but sophomore year on, I got stuck babysitting my sister after school." My mom used to work from home, but she got a new boss that year who decided everyone needed to come into the office. My sister was too young to be left alone, so I had to watch her until one of my parents got back. "I shouldn't be penalized for that—it's not fair."

Ms. Vail nodded. "You can definitely include babysitting, but what about other activities? Like writing for the school newspaper or the literary magazine, volunteering to plant trees on the weekends, being an office worker during your study halls, signing up for the cleanup committee for the school dances? There are plenty of options that don't involve staying after the last bell."

I hadn't even thought of those things. My heartbeat quickened. I was busy all the time; there had to be stuff that would qualify as an extracurricular. "I'm at almost every nighttime soccer game," I said, letting the words tumble out, "and a ton of the volleyball ones. And now that my sister is older, and I don't need to be home, I'll be going to the afternoon games, too. I even have one today. I'm like their number one cheerleader."

"But you're not a cheerleader, you're a spectator, and that doesn't make for a compelling application."

I didn't need to be on the cheerleading team to show I had school spirit—anyone who saw me at the games knew that—but Ms. Vail clearly disagreed.

"Okay then, how about this. I, um, helped at the soccer team's car wash. I manned a booth at my synagogue's Purim carnival. I . . ." I couldn't think of anything else. Unless hanging out with your best friends and your boyfriend a ridiculous amount counted for something.

"Cam . . ."

"Oh," I said, clapping my hands together, "the yearbook!"

"You were on yearbook?" she asked, flipping through the pages of her CAMRYN ROTH file.

"Not technically, but last year they told people to send in their photos, and I'm always taking pictures, so I submitted a bunch. They used a few, and they would have taken more, if there had been seniors in them instead of my group of friends. But I can still write down yearbook photographer, right?"

Ms. Vail pursed her lips. "Cam, I'm not the admissions board. I'm not the one you're going to need to convince. I'm just trying to prepare you. The way things look now, I think you need to seriously consider some other options. I'm afraid you may not be able to get into Columbia."

The bell rang, interrupting us, but I didn't get up. I didn't budge. I was frozen to my chair. I could hear students racing out of classrooms with that rush of excitement that comes with leaving school on a Friday—and not just *any* Friday. The *first* Friday of the school year.

"Can you stay a few extra minutes?" Ms. Vail asked, once the ringing stopped.

I nodded. I wasn't going anywhere, not until we fixed this mess.

"Reading," I said, reaching into my backpack and pulling out three books I had stashed there. "I do it all the time. I took these out of the library right before lunch. I've probably taken out more books than anyone at this school. Ms. Chakrabarti can vouch for me—I'd bet she would even write me a recommendation." I knew

I was grasping at straws, but how come kicking a ball counted as an extracurricular, but reading—which was so much more mind opening—didn't count?

I droned on and on about my favorite romances to my friends. I'd pretty much given a dissertation about the differences between the book *Simon vs. the Homo Sapiens Agenda* and the movie *Love, Simon*. They'd tuned me out, but maybe, possibly, that counted as a book club? I'd take any sort of win at the moment.

"I don't want you to worry," Ms. Vail continued. "There are plenty of excellent schools you can get into. Why don't we take a look at some of those?"

Because I didn't want any of those.

Columbia had been my dream forever.

I was so ready to leave this small town and be in a big city. Ever since my aunt took me to Manhattan in fifth grade, I'd wanted to go back. I hadn't had a chance, thanks to my parents' fear of me traveling to the city sans chaperone, but by some miracle they were okay with me applying to school there. I couldn't wait, and Columbia seemed like the perfect school for me.

Marc was the one who first got me excited about it. He was a legacy. His grandma and both of his parents had gone there, and his older brother was enrolled now. The way Marc talked about the campus, the classes, the prestige, and the city had made me fall in love with it—enough that I'd worked my butt off to get straight As so that I could get in.

Ever since freshman year, the two of us had planned to go to Columbia together. It was a pact sealed with a kiss. Cheesy, I know, but the thought still made me grin like a fool. Marc was a shoo-in to get accepted. Not only did he have the family connections, but he didn't have any extracurricular deficiencies. Marc was a star athlete, on the student senate, and took all AP classes—which he aced. Apparently, unbeknownst to me until a few minutes ago, *I* was the slacker.

I was the one jeopardizing everything.

No. I shook my head. I wasn't giving up. I had worked too hard to not get into my dream school.

"I still have time. I can fix this," I told Ms. Vail. She knew how persistent I was; she'd gotten a taste of it over the summer. Now I was going to multiply my efforts tenfold. Sure, this squashed any hope of applying early decision, but that was okay. The extra time would help get me where I needed to be. "You'll see. I'll get incredible recommendations, keep my grades up, and find some extracurriculars. I'll do whatever it takes. I can make this happen. Columbia will be laying out the red carpet by the time I'm through."

Ms. Vail gave me one of those pitying smiles I could never stand. "I hope you're right. But you only have two marking periods before applications are due. That's not a lot of time."

"I'll make it work."

I had to.

Everything I dreamed about depended on it.

Chapter 2

I opened the door to the gymnasium, careful not to bring any attention to myself. I was super late. The volleyball match was well underway. I glanced up at the scoreboard and cringed. It wasn't good. Fourth set, and Brooksvale was down. They needed to tie this game to stay alive. Grace and her teammates broke out of a huddle and took their spots on the court. They looked intense. I scanned the bleachers for my other best friend, Terri Marin, and quickly maneuvered my way through the stands to her.

Her dark eyes were focused on her sketch pad, her long brown-almost-black curls hanging over the page, as the pencil in her hand moved at warp speed. I snapped a photo with my phone. I'd call it *The Artist at Work*. Terri didn't notice me do it; she was so fixated on her drawing that she didn't even stir when I sat down next to her. "Hey," I said, bumping my shoulder gently into hers. "Sorry I'm late. Got stuck at the guidance counselor's office. Long, horrible story. I'll tell you all about it."

She turned toward me, and before she could even get out a word, my mouth dropped into an O and I gasped. "Oh no. Don't kill me." I squeezed my eyes shut. "I'm so, so sorry. I did not do this on purpose. I meant to change. Honest. I totally forgot with everything that happened." I peeked one eye open. "How mad are you?"

Terri was shaking her head and pinching her navy-blue shirt, which had a giant *GO* written on it in silver glitter. "How many times did you make me promise I would remember to put this on?" she asked.

"Eight?" I answered, scrunching my nose.

"Try fifteen," she corrected me. "And yet, somehow, I'm the one looking like a glitter bomb exploded on me, while Little Miss School Spirit is wearing plain old jeans and a lacy pink top. Not even wearing school colors. You're slipping."

Fortunately, her voice seemed playful and not pissed. Still, I felt guilty. "I wasn't even thinking. I can go get mine. It's in my locker." The shirt I was supposed to be wearing had Grace's name written on it in the same silver glitter.

Terri shook her head. "Forget it. By the time you get back here, the whole match will be over. But you owe me! I have sparkles everywhere. I'll probably still be dripping glitter at graduation." She picked a piece off her arm to emphasize her point.

"I totally owe you." I put up my fingers in the Girl Scout Promise. "On my honor, I promise to help Terri at all times, and to live by the Girl Scout Law," I recited, altering the organization's pledge.

"That's a start," Terri said, but she was already back to sketching in her pad, which meant I was off the hook. When Terri was angry, she made sure you knew it.

"On the plus side, you're wearing my art," I reminded her. "That should make you happy."

She raised an eyebrow at me. "You definitely need Winters' class if you think this shirt is art."

"Hey," I said, crossing my arms over my chest and putting on my best mock-indignation voice. "The Griffin kids and I worked very hard on that. Wait until you see the signs we made."

"Hopefully, the twins made them by themselves. I've seen your work." She laughed at her own joke.

The Griffins were five-year-olds I babysat every once in a while. Terri did, too. The kids loved doing any type of crafts project. Unfortunately, my skills were pretty much on par with theirs, which everyone seemed to be reminding me about today.

"We can't all be Picasso," I told her.

"Picasso, really? Surrealism or neoclassical—you really think that's my style?"

I threw my hands up. "You just told me a kindergartener is more artistic than I am—do you really think I know the difference between periods or styles?"

"Yes. I mean, I know all about rom-coms, and the romance tropes you go on and on about." She started ticking them off on her fingers. "Friends to lovers. Enemies to lovers. Second-chance romance. Destined lov—"

"Okay, okay, I get it, you're a better listener than I am. But in my defense, you usually talk about your inspiration for a piece—i.e., a hot guy, a memory, Christmas tinsel—and not your particular style. Besides, you know I'm your biggest fan. Well, other than Luke." I wiggled my eyebrows up and down.

"Oh my God, don't go there—you know we're just friends," Terri said, swatting me with her sketch pad.

I grabbed it. She and Luke Cahill had gone out a couple of times during sophomore year, but it never went anywhere. Terri thought that being in a long-term relationship in high school was stupid, that tying yourself down was for when you were old and boring. At first, it didn't seem like Luke felt the same way. He was always hanging around us, but eventually he kind of became one of us—an honorary member of our little group, even if I did like to tease Terri about their dating history every once in a while.

"Terri," I moaned, her current sketch catching my eye, "please tell me your motivation for this one isn't Lissi." I whispered the name, even though Grace was nowhere near us. "Grace is going to have a fit."

"It's not my fault," Terri said, grabbing her pad back. "Look how intense her expression is. It hasn't changed throughout the whole game. How could I not draw that?"

I followed Terri's gaze to the sidelines. There was Lissi. I hadn't noticed her, but now that I did, it *was* hard to look away. She was hyperfocused on the game. She was leaning forward, lips pursed, eyes lasered in on the players. "Nice ace!" Lissi called out after Crystal Pollack made a serve that the other team couldn't return. "Do it again."

"Well, the sight of Grace's fists might be a deterrent," I said, noticing the way her arm muscles were bulging.

Grace's hands were tight balls, and her whole body was stiff. She looked like a force to be reckoned with. Lissi either didn't notice or didn't care, because she went right on shouting out instructions. Apparently, she had been a star on her team back in New Hampshire. But here in Brooksvale, that role belonged to Grace. She had worked hard to bring the team together, to keep everyone in sync, and to make practice a priority. She'd been bumped up to varsity during sophomore year and helped turn a losing team into state champions. This year she was finally captain, and she loved all nineteen of her teammates.

Our varsity teams could only roster twenty players each, and the volleyball team was full. But according to Grace, Lissi showed up at summer practice for the last two weeks, right before school started, and said she wanted to be on the team. Coach was hesitant to make an exception. If you let one extra on, why not two or three, or ten, or everyone who tried out? He wanted a team he could manage—and coach properly. JV was for the masses, at least at Brooksvale. Allowing Lissi on would mean kicking someone else off. There was still a discussion about what to do. In the meantime, Lissi kept attending practices, and now apparently the games. This annoyed Grace to no end.

"You might want to burn that picture before Grace sees it," I warned Terri.

"I think you might be right," she said, turning to a fresh page in her pad. "So why were you so late today? What happened with the guidance counselor?"

Instead of answering, I jumped out of my seat. "Go, Grace!" I screamed, and started clapping. She had just spiked the ball over the net, winning the set and tying the match. It was 2–2. Anyone's game.

"Come on," I said, pulling Terri's arm.

Terri gathered up all her stuff. "This is the most ridiculous thing ever."

She said that every time, but it was tradition. At Brooksvale High volleyball games, when the teams switched sides, so did the spectators.

I took her bag from her. "You don't want Grace thinking you're rooting for her opponents."

Terri's face went wooden. "Trust me. She knows if I'm at a game, I'm here for her."

"You're a good friend," I told her, patting her on the back. Terri was not shy about her disdain for sports. But she rarely missed Grace's home games. She was one of those people you could always count on to be there.

"I know," Terri said with a smirk as she climbed down the bleachers.

As we neared the other side of the gym, some guy I'd never seen gave a meek wave.

"Terri, hi."

She winked at him and kept walking, adding just a smidge more sway to her hips. Terri was curvy and confident, and I was more than a little in awe of her ability to flirt and make friends wherever she went.

"Who was that?" I whispered.

"Remember I told you about Mr. Sneezed-All-Over-My-Pizza?" she said as we situated ourselves in our new seats. "That was him."

"No way." I totally remembered that story. Terri had met some guy at a Sandbrook High party; they ditched it and went out for a slice, and as they were sitting outside eating, he sneezed all over hers. "That was *him*?"

"Yes," she said, giving me eyes that said *don't you dare look in his direction*, "but that was a million years ago. Who cares?" It was actually only about five months, but who was counting? "Are you going to answer my question or what?" she continued.

"Huh?"

"What happened with the guidance counselor?"

"Oh yeah." I sighed and then filled her in about my lack of extracurriculars, and how if I didn't find some soon, my Columbia dreams would be over.

Terri shook her head. "I told you not to quit volleyball over a boy."

"I didn't. I did it to watch my sister."

She gave me another one of her stares—she was the queen of them—and this particular look always had me spilling the truth whether I wanted to or not. "Okay, fine. I did it for a boy. But not for just *any* boy—for Marc." I could tell she had to resist rolling her eyes. I quit the volleyball team before the end of the season during my freshman year so I could watch Marc play in the soccer finals. He was so excited about getting that far, and I didn't want to miss his moment. "But it wasn't like I was that great, and I would have had to quit the next year anyway."

"You're always doing what Marc—" She stopped herself. "I'm sorry. This isn't the time for that." She squeezed my arm. "You're amazing, Cam. I know how much you want to get into Columbia. You'll figure something out. And if you need anything, I'm here to help."

"Thanks."

"What did Marc say about your meeting?"

I pressed my hands down on the bleacher. "Nothing yet. By the time I was done with the guidance counselor, he was already in soccer practice. He won't look at his phone for hours." Although I knew his first words were going to be that it would all work out. It wasn't necessarily true, but hearing him say it would make me feel better anyway. It always did. I really needed to talk to him. "I'll see him tonight; we're going to the diner. Hopefully, he'll be able to come up with something."

"*You'll* be able to."

I let the statement go. I knew Terri wasn't the biggest Marc Gerber fan. She thought I relied on him too much, but that was because she didn't understand what it was like to be in a couple.

Marc and I were better together. What we had wasn't boring or mutually dependent—it was love. And with him by my side, there was no way I couldn't get through this.

I was more determined than ever. I was going to Columbia, and so was Marc. We just needed a new plan.

Chapter 3

It had only been a few hours since my meeting with my guidance counselor, but in that time I'd gone from stressed to panicked. "Whoa," the waitress said as I inhaled the last remnants of my Oreo Madness shake through my straw. "That was fast. Want another?"

I looked up from my book and shook my head no. I could have done without the commentary, but I bit my tongue. Tonight was definitely a two-, possibly three-shake night. Still, I was going to wait until Marc got there before I dove into my next one.

We were supposed to meet at Scobell's Diner at seven, but I'd arrived a half hour early. I needed to get out of my house, so I had my mom drive me over as soon as she could. I was feeling antsy. The volleyball game had been a temporary distraction, but I couldn't shake Ms. Vail's words. Thoughts of Marc were the only things calming me down.

I couldn't even focus on my book. I'd read the same page six times, and I was at my favorite part—where the dorky yet adorable main character was about to learn that her secret crush actually liked her. *Loved* her, even. Their eyes would meet; they'd move closer until they were mere millimeters apart. Then they'd have that epic kiss, the one to seal their fate as a perfect couple, so that they could ride off into their happily-ever-after. Except that this time it wasn't cheering me up. All I could think about was that my perfect ending had a giant crack in it and was in serious danger of falling apart. Sure, not going to the same college as Marc wouldn't destroy us, but it would make things a lot harder. I wanted things to be easy and fun. My dream school with my dream guy. I closed the book and put it back in my bag. Why couldn't life be like a rom-com?

I took a deep breath.

The clock above the cash register ticked to seven, but it didn't magically make my boyfriend appear. Not that I was surprised—he was never on time. Sometimes I'd tell him things started twenty minutes earlier than they actually did, just so he'd get there when I wanted him to. I hoped today he wouldn't keep me waiting too long. I really needed to see his face.

I played with my straw and scanned the crowd. Scobell's was busy. I guess that was to be expected since it was the first Friday night of the school year. The diner was swamped on a normal evening—it was pretty much the main hangout for every high school kid in Brooksvale, Sandbrook, and every other surrounding town— and after having to deal with homework and classes after a whole summer off, everyone wanted to go out. I recognized a bunch of faces, not that I really knew them—just *of* them. A couple of people from the newspaper were there. Some guy Terri had hung out with for like a week during sophomore year was sitting with a group I didn't know. Grace's old chem lab partner was at the table behind me. And Avery Owens and her cheerleading clique were by the old arcade games. She looked up, had probably sensed me staring, but I turned my focus back to my phone before she could catch my eye. I didn't want to seem like some stalker.

Right as I was about to text Marc, he walked in the door. He was wearing his faded blue Yankees T-shirt. I couldn't help but smile at the familiar sight. He wore that thing all the time. I'd bought him a new team shirt for his birthday, but he wouldn't give up that old one. He said he wore it during a game where the Yankees had an epic comeback, and that it was "lucky." Marc was about as attached to it as my little sister was to her security blanket—even though at thirteen she was way too old for it. Hopefully, the shirt would conjure up some magic and help us figure out this whole Columbia mess.

I caught Marc's eye; he nodded at me and held up a finger to indicate "one minute" as he stopped by a table over by the far wall. I leaned over to get a better look. It was a bunch of the guys from the soccer team. I wished I had seen them earlier; I totally would have sat with them while I waited. I couldn't make out what they were saying, but a couple of minutes later Marc slid into the booth across from me.

"Hey," he said.

"Hey." I reached out and took his hand. He was still tan from the summer, his usual pale complexion sun-kissed. I hated that I hadn't gotten to spend the past few months with him. He was always happiest when the weather was warm.

Marc stared down at the table, and his messy dark brown curls tumbled forward. The familiar scent of coconut-scented shampoo and musky body spray flooded my nose. I took a deep whiff. Some people liked to breathe in lavender and jasmine to calm down, but my go-to scent was Marc. Being with him was exactly what I needed right now.

"I'm so glad you're here. I've been freaking out ever since I left the guidance counselor. I even went off on my mom on the way over here. She kept asking what we were doing tonight, and I just lost it." I puffed my cheeks with air and let my breath out slowly. "'It's a diner, we're eating, what do you think,'" I said, giving a playback of my response—sarcastic tone and all. I felt guilty. I shouldn't have taken it out on my mom. I just hadn't been in a talking mood.

"I wouldn't worry about it," Marc said, his eyes still focused on the table. "I'm sure she's over it."

He wouldn't even look at me. We hadn't talked since I'd texted him the news, and he seemed to be taking it even harder than I had. With my free hand, I tossed my straw wrapper at him. "Hey, you okay?"

"Yeah. It's just . . ." Marc's voice trailed off.

He didn't have to say anything. I understood. This Columbia thing was screwing everything up. "It will be all right. It's us. And I'm going to do whatever I can to make sure I get in." Somehow I'd wound up trying to comfort *him* instead of the other way around, but I couldn't help it. I hated seeing him upset. It snapped me into Miss Fix-It mode. "Now let's brainstorm." I squeezed his hand. "I need that mind of yours."

Before we got the chance, the waitress came over. "Get you guys anything?"

"I think we're going to need two extra-large Mint Explosion milk—"

"Actually," Marc said, cutting me off, "can you give us a few minutes? We might be heading out soon."

I put my other hand on his and practically bounced in my seat. "Ooh. This sounds good. What do you have in mind? Where are we going? What are we doing?" I knew I sounded like an overeager kindergartener, but I didn't care. This was what I'd been craving. A Marc pick-me-up. Some sort of special surprise that would make me feel like all of this would be okay again.

"Cam . . ." He looked up, his hazel eyes locking onto mine.

He looked so sad.

"Marc, please don't stress. You're going to make me stress. It's going to work out. I can feel it."

He pulled his hands back and started rubbing his neck.

I winked at him. "Need some help? I give a pretty mean massage."

Marc shook his head. "No, I'm okay."

He was *okay*? Marc never turned down a massage. Half the time, he begged for them. "Now you're really freaking me out."

He swallowed, his Adam's apple bobbing in his throat. "It's just . . . I was thinking . . . maybe this isn't such a bad thing."

My stomach turned, the milkshake lying heavy. "What?"

His eyes flitted from me to my empty cup and stayed there. "Going to different schools. Maybe it's better if we don't do college together. Do you really even want to go to Columbia? Or even New York?"

My whole body tensed up. I couldn't be hearing him right; we'd talked about this since freshman year. He knew I'd always wanted to be in Manhattan. And, sure, going to Columbia together had been *his* idea, but it was one that I had wholeheartedly fallen in love with. "Yes, I want to. What's gotten into you? I'm not giving up on our dream. Don't let Ms. Vail make you all paranoid. I'm going to get in. Besides, do you know how hard long distance would be? I don't even want to think about it."

"Yeah," he said, his voice sounding far away. Then he paused. It was just a few seconds, but it seemed like hours, and my whole body somehow felt hot and cold at the same time. "That's why . . . um . . . maybe it would be better for both of us if we kind of ended things now."

I couldn't move. I couldn't think.

Kind of ended things now? Had he just broken up with me?

In a diner?

No. He wouldn't.

"What?" I asked, or at least I think I asked. My mouth opened, it formed the word, but I didn't hear any sound come out.

This time Marc took my hand and said, "Maybe we should each do our own thing. It's our senior year."

I snapped my hand away from his. *Our own thing?* What did that even mean? "Are you breaking up with me?" I managed to croak out.

"Don't call it that. It's more like . . . I'm doing what's best for both of us."

This wasn't what was *best*. It was the exact opposite.

Everything got foggy. I could see Marc in front of me, but it felt like he was miles away.

He kept talking.

"I mean, this summer, didn't you like having some space? A chance to be on your own?"

My mouth opened, but this time I couldn't get any words out. I just stared at him.

Over the summer, I had been a counselor at an overnight camp in Massachusetts. I'd hated being away from him. I snuck phone calls and texts whenever I could. Marc had always said he missed me, too.

"This will be good for both of us, don't you think?" he asked, looking at me now and nodding, as if that would make me agree.

"You've got to be kidding me," I answered, finding my voice. "Good!? Obviously, I don't think this will be *good*."

"Cam, come on."

The more he spoke, the angrier I got. "What would make you think I'd find anything about this good? You're ruining everything. Don't you see that?"

He put out his hands and lowered them slowly, looking around, embarrassed.

I stared at him. Was he trying to shush me? "What?" I asked.

"Keep it down," he whispered. "People are starting to look."

I dug my fingers into the red pleather cushion I was sitting on. I had no idea how loud I was being, and I didn't care. My volume was not my main concern, and it shouldn't have been his, either. "Seriously? Tell me you're joking," I said, digging my nails in deeper. I was still trying to comprehend that the guy I'd been in love with forever was calling it quits out of nowhere, and he was critiquing my *volume*?

"Please don't make a scene."

"You're worried about a scene. A *SCENE*." Somehow I found myself standing, my hands slapping the table in front of me. "You dump me *here*, now, and *that's* what you're worried about?"

He was standing now, too. "You want this all over the internet?" He waved his arms around the room. "Because that's what's happening," he said in a harsh whisper. "Look at all the phones out." He clucked his tongue. "I should have known you'd do something like this."

Something in me snapped. "Me? ME! What is wrong with *you*? We've been together for years, Marc. *Years*. How did you think I'd react?"

He ran his hand through his hair. "You know what, if this is how it's going to be, if we can't talk like normal people, I'm out of here. You're acting like a—"

"Watch it, Marc," Avery Owens called out as she moved from the cheerleaders' table and toward us. "I'd be very careful about what you say next."

He rolled his eyes at her.

Tears were threatening to escape my eyes, but I fought them back. "Marc, please, just sit down," I told him. I needed answers; I needed to know what had happened. If he wanted me to be quiet, I would. I'd do anything if it meant he'd stay. "Please," I said, my voice almost a whisper, but he didn't seem to care.

"You know what, let's do this another time. We'll talk tomorrow or something. This was a mistake."

It *was* a mistake. This whole thing was, but I couldn't wait a whole day to talk to him. I needed answers *now*. My thoughts were already racing. Twenty-four hours from now, I'd be going out of my mind. This was all I was going to be able to think about. He had to stay and hash it out. Was he really going to leave me here?

He moved out of the booth.

"Marc!" I cried out.

He turned to go. He might have made it, too, except he almost smacked right into Avery.

"She asked you to sit down," she quietly hissed, her brown eyes lasering into his.

"This is none of your business, Avery," he said.

"No kidding," she told him. "But you made it my business, *every-one's* business, when you broke up with your girlfriend of two—"

"Three," I corrected her.

"Three years," she continued, "in the middle of a crowded diner. If she wants you to sit, you sit. If she wants you to leave, you leave. This isn't about you anymore." He looked like he was going to say something, but then he actually slunk back into our booth. Avery turned to the crowd. "And the rest of you put away the phones and go back to eating your food. What is wrong with everyone?"

For the briefest instant, my grief turned to awe as I watched her.

"Are you okay?" she asked me.

I nodded.

"If you need *anything*," Avery said, "anything at all, I'm right over there." She pointed to her booth.

"Thanks."

She nodded slightly, but I could tell she meant what she said. Her words were sincere.

After Avery walked away, Marc asked, "Do you want to go somewhere else and talk?"

I shook my head. That would have been a great question before all of this had started, but now I didn't have the energy. I just wanted answers.

"Why did you do this here?" I asked him, wiping my eyes with my arm, leaving a trail of black eyeliner. I didn't want him to see me crying, not when he was acting all indifferent. "It was cruel."

His tone changed. I'm not sure if it was what I said, what Avery had said, or that he was afraid people were still watching, but his voice got soft, like he was trying to calm an animal that had escaped from the zoo. "I thought it would be easier."

But I wasn't some wild animal. *I* was a human being with feelings. Feelings he didn't care about, or he never would have done this—not here, not at all. I let out a maniacal laugh. "Easier for who? You? Because if you haven't noticed, it's not easier for me."

"Cam," he said.

I held up my hand to stop him. "No, don't. You thought if you did it here, you could just get it over with, not have to deal with the mess, or even think about it. It's not going to be that easy." So much for not crying in front of him. The tears began streaming down my cheeks.

"Please don't cry," Marc said and pulled out a napkin from the holder and handed it to me.

Please don't cry? PLEASE DON'T CRY? The guy I love, the guy who said he loved me, just told me it's over, and he wants me to what? Smile?

I took the napkin and blew my nose. "Why are you doing this? What changed?" I choked out, the anger giving way to hurt.

He slunk down even farther in the booth and let out a sigh. "Nothing. Everything. We've been together for all of high school. And we're seniors now . . . and . . . I don't know, I just thought it could be fun not to be in a relationship."

The words felt like a knife twisting in my gut. "*Fun?* So, what, you want to date other people?"

"I don't know what I want, and maybe that's the problem. I want to figure it out. It was like I got to breathe this summer while you were gone, and—"

I squeezed my eyes shut. "I was *choking* you?"

"No, you're twisting my words. Cam, I love you, I do. You know that."

He sure had a funny way of showing it. This wasn't how you treated someone you loved. "I don't know that. Not anymore."

His eyebrows furrowed. "I do—it's just . . . I don't want this right now. But this doesn't have to be goodbye. I don't want to lose you altogether. We can still be—"

"Don't say it." If he said the word *friends*, I was going to explode. I wanted to be his *girl*friend. Not his pal.

"I'm sorry," he said.

We sat there in silence. Part of me hoped he'd realize he was making a horrible mistake. Part of me wanted to scream. The other part was just too drained to do anything.

I felt a shadow cloud over our table, and I looked up. Vern Harmon, one of Marc's soccer buddies—and a guy I thought was my friend, too—was standing over us. He didn't even glance in my direction. "A bunch of us are getting out of here," he told Marc. "You coming?"

Marc looked from Vern to me, silently asking for my permission to leave this hell.

"Just go," I said.

He didn't argue, or even check if I was okay. He just jumped out of the booth and booked it for the exit.

I watched him go, watched the door close behind him.

Marc left.

He had left *me*, and he wasn't coming back.

I covered my face with my hands and sobbed.

Marc and I were over.

Chapter 4

A hand touched my shoulder. I held my breath. Thank God, Marc had come back! He must have realized how awful he was being and what a mistake he was making. I lowered my hands, ready to work everything out, to give him hell for putting me through this but to eventually, inevitably, forgive him and get back to where we were before.

Only it wasn't Marc who had come to comfort me.

It was Avery.

A virtual stranger cared more about my well-being than the guy I would have done anything for. It made me sob even harder. I didn't care that Avery was watching. That *everyone* was watching. There was no hiding the fact that my life was falling apart.

"It's going to be okay. *You're* going to be okay," Avery said. "Is it all right if I sit?"

I nodded. I really didn't want to be around anyone, but I really didn't want to be alone, either.

She put a glass down in front of me. "I brought you some water."

I reached for it but stopped midway. I was visibly shaking. I was an even bigger mess than I thought. I managed to get the glass to my lips, take a sip, and put it down. Then I watched my fingers tremble. Avery put her hand over mine. "What do you say we get out of here? Do you want me to call someone for you? Help you to your car? Whatever you need."

More sobs bubbled to the surface. I couldn't go anywhere. "Marc was my ride."

My mom had dropped me off, but she and my dad were going out as soon as she got home. My *boyfriend* was supposed to make sure I got back. Now I was going to have to wait for my parents or risk their wrath and take a Lyft or Uber. They didn't trust the apps, but I wasn't sure I cared.

"I can take you," Avery offered.

I shook my head. "You don't have to." I didn't want to be anybody's charity case.

"I want to. Please."

I studied her face. She looked sincere, and I really had nothing to lose. I stood up and followed Avery to her car.

"It's unlocked," she said.

Once I was inside, I leaned my head against the window. It was throbbing.

"I'm so stupid."

"No you're not."

There was no way that was true. I'd had no idea that my own boyfriend was planning to dump me. We'd hung out when I got back from camp, I had sat with him at lunch every day we'd been in school, we'd joked around, even kissed in art class, and yet I'd had no inkling he was about to turn everything upside down. Sure sounded stupid to me.

"He should be the one feeling miserable," Avery insisted, "not you."

I closed my eyes. I appreciated what she was trying to do, but it wasn't going to change anything. *I* was the one with tears in my eyes. *I* was the one who felt like a stack of bricks had landed on my chest. *I* was the one who didn't know what do with myself. Marc was off having a night out with his friends, enjoying his *freedom*. The miserable award went to me—warranted or not.

"Um, Cam," Avery said a little while later. It could have been seconds, minutes, hours; I'd lost track. All I could think about was Marc. Our conversation played on repeat in my brain.

I raised my head in her direction.

"Your address?" she asked quietly.

Right. Of course. I gave it to her, and we drove the rest of the way in silence.

She parked the car, and I fumbled with the seat belt. "Thanks," I told her. I didn't know what else to say, so I just opened the door and got out.

Avery did, too. "You said your parents weren't home, right? How about I keep you company for a bit?"

"You don't have to."

She shrugged her shoulder. "I don't mind. You shouldn't be alone."

Alone.

But that's what I was. There was no more coupledom for me. I *was* on my own. I probably needed to get used to it. Avery was watching me, and I tensed as I thought about everything she—and the rest of the diner—had witnessed.

A giant scene in the middle of Scobell's, starring me.

Now Avery was ready for the sequel. What did she want from me? Was she just trying to help? Was she afraid I was going to do something stupid? Did she want a story, some good gossip to tell her cheerleading buddies? "My sister's home. I'll be fine," I said, unable to get that last thought out of my mind. Was she going to get back into her car and text everyone she knew about what a pathetic loser I was?

"Why are you doing this for me anyway?" I asked. Then I shook my head. I'd just snapped at the only person who had been nice to me, the only one at the diner who'd checked how I was doing. "Sorry, I just . . ." I didn't finish. Avery had been nothing but kind. I hadn't meant to be rude. Why did I keep taking things out on the wrong people? "I'm sorry."

"Don't be," she said. "I get it. It's not like we're friends or anything. I just saw Marc being an ass, and I thought you could use someone on your side. I'd want someone on mine."

My eyes filled up again. Marc used to be the one on my side. Not the one I needed saving from.

"He never should have done that in there," she went on, her eyes getting a faraway look. "Getting dumped sucks. Trust me, I know." Avery and Scottie Zhang had ended things last May. Seeing her after it happened, I'd always thought she was the one who'd done the breaking up. She seemed so happy. It never even crossed my mind that it could have been an act or that she was hurting. She focused her attention back on me. "We girls need to stick together, right?"

I nodded. "Thank you. I really don't deserve this." I felt guilty. I barely spoke to Avery, or any of the cheerleaders, for that matter, even though I had classes with most of them. I thought they were snobby because of the way they were always huddled together, laughing and whispering. But I guess it was no different from how my friends and I behaved.

My rom-coms apparently didn't get everything right. Not all

pretty, popular cheerleaders were cruel. In fact, it would seem some were secretly Wonder Woman coming to the aid of heartbroken souls at local diners.

Avery put up her hand. "Stop. You do deserve this."

There she was, being all amazing again.

I reached into my bag to get out my keys, and noticed my phone. "Whoa." It was blowing up. Hundreds of messages were waiting for me, most of them from Grace. If she was going for the Guinness World Record for Most Texts Sent in Under Thirty Minutes, she was well on her way to succeeding.

I scrolled through the messages.

GRACE
Omg, Cam. I'm so sorry. Are you OK?

Marc totally sucks.

I'm with Terri. Please let us know you're all right.

"Grace and Terri are freaking out," I told Avery. Then I realized what that meant. My news had spread beyond the diner and to the rest of the school.

"Cam?" Avery asked, waving her hand in front of my face. "Cam?"

I shook myself back to life. "I'm fine." It was a lie, but maybe if I said it enough, it would be true. My breakup was all over the internet for everyone to see. It had felt real before, but this made it seem permanent.

I looked back at my phone.

> **GRACE**
> OK, you don't have to answer, just don't move.
> We're coming to the diner to pick you up.

Too late on that one. I was about to respond when I saw what she wrote next.

> **GRACE**
> They told us Avery gave you a
> ride home. We're coming.

> Oh, and Terri says you'd have more texts from
> her if she wasn't driving, and that she thinks
> Marc is the biggest jerk on the planet.

> Now she wants me to tell you that wasn't
> her wording, and that I am censoring her
> creative curse words for that @$!*$@&*
> ex of yours. Yeah, you know I can't type
> what she said. We'll be there soon.

The tears that had been threatening to escape finally did.

"What happened?" Avery asked, her eyes widening. "Was it Marc? Did he say something?"

"No, it was Grace. She and Terri are on their way."

"Then why are you crying?"

I wiped my face with my arm. "It's just them. You. This day has been crappy, but you've all been—" Another huge sob escaped. "Sorry, I'm not always this big of a crier."

"Stop apologizing. Come on," Avery said, linking her elbow with mine. "I'll wait with you until your friends get here."

I let her lead me to the door.

This day still royally sucked, but it had some bright spots—some bright people, who were watching out for me and helping me to keep moving—and that was something. Maybe I wasn't alone after all.

Chapter 5

"Why are you home already?" my sister, Jemma, asked as little pieces of potato chips fell from her mouth.

"You're disgusting," I told her.

She was sitting on the floor in front of the TV, a giant bag of Lay's to her left, a two-liter bottle of Coke in front of her, and boxes of Swedish Fish, M&M's, and Twizzlers to her right. If she kept this up, there was a good chance my parents would make me start staying home to babysit her again.

"And you're not supposed to be here." She looked from me to Avery and back again. "Weren't you supposed to be hanging out with Marc?" Her nose scrunched up as she scrutinized what had to be my red-rimmed eyes. "Where is he?"

"Dead," I said, expressionless.

Her eyes widened to about twice their size. "What! Oh my God. What happened?"

"Relax—"

"How can I relax?" She jumped up, cutting me off before I could explain. "He's *dead*!"

"Oh my God." I shook my head. Obviously, I wasn't being serious. She had to know that. "Will you calm down? He's not *dead* dead. He's dead to me."

Jemma crossed her arms, and one single, surely fabricated tear dripped down her cheek. "That wasn't funny, Caaaammmrrrryyyyynnnn." She dragged out the syllables in my name for what felt like half an eternity. And everyone thought I was the dramatic one? They clearly did not spend enough time with my little sister. "You don't joke about things like that. It's not funny. At. All. Think how you'd feel if something actually happened to him." Then she stormed off in a huff, her frizzy reddish-brown hair, identical to mine, whipping around her.

"I'm sorry!" I yelled out after her. Even though I knew she was just reacting for show, I still felt guilty. Great, another thing to feel bad about.

I picked up her stash of snacks. "Regretting your decision to come over?" I asked Avery.

"Nah, I'm sure I was worse to my big brother when I was her age."

"I doubt it." I nodded toward the steps. "Let's go upstairs. Jemma will be back down soon, and I can't deal with her right now."

I led the way to my room.

"Whoa," Avery said as she stepped inside.

"Oh," I said, following her gaze. "That's my picture wall."

"I can see that," she said, walking over to it.

There were hundreds of photos taped there. I was all for posting on social media, but there was something about a physical picture that I loved. I'd started the collage when I moved to Brooksvale in second grade, to remember everyone I left back in Shaker Heights, Ohio. But in the many years since, images of Terri, Grace, me—and *Marc*—pretty much ruled the wall.

As Avery looked over the pictures hanging by my desk, I climbed onto my bed and studied the ones taped up right by my pillow. They were the last things I saw before I went to sleep every night and the first things when I woke up every morning.

"No, no, no, no, no, no," Avery said as I traced my favorite picture with my fingers. It was one of Marc and me roasting marshmallows out on the beach last year. I was looking at the fire, but he was looking at me. His gaze was pure love. At least that's what I had thought. I had a whole little section of the wall for just the two of us.

"You don't want him," Avery reminded me, and gently threw a stuffed koala bear sitting at the edge of my bed in my direction.

I hugged it to my chest. But *I did.*

My expression must have been easy to read because she continued. "*Trust me*, you don't."

She was making sense. My head knew that, but my heart was having a harder time getting the message.

Avery grabbed scissors from my desk and marched over to me. "You know what to do," she said, holding them out.

I did, but that didn't mean I wanted to. "Do I have to?"

"I'm not going to force you . . . ," she said, still waiting for me to take them. "But do you really want to look at his face every single day? Every single *night?*"

Yes.

That was the wrong answer. I knew that, and staring at his face wasn't going to help me get over him. I plucked the scissors from her. This was a rite of passage that I'd seen more times than I could count. Any breakup film worth its weight had some sort of ritual cleansing: cutting photos, burning reminders of an ex, something! Sure, the symbolism was cliché—getting rid of things from the past to make room for the future—but there was truth to it. Those scenes always made me smile. And I definitely needed a smile.

I pulled a couple of photos down. Except that feeling of closure didn't wash over me. It made me feel emptier than before, if that was even possible. "This sucks." I held the picture of Marc and me at my sweet sixteen, his arm draped around my waist. "I looked so happy in this one."

"So snip out his face. Keep you. You can put your dream guy on there instead."

"Marc is my—"

Avery cut me off. "Don't say it. A guy who would treat you like *he* treated you is not a dream guy."

She was right.

I looked at the picture one last time and then plunged the scissors in.

It was time to cut Marc Gerber out of my life.

Chapter 6

I jumped when footsteps charged toward my room. Moments later my sister was facing me, hands on hips and green eyes in slits. "More company for you. Do Mom and Dad know you're having this many people over? It's not fair—they wouldn't even let me have one person hang out, and you're practically having a party."

Before I could answer, Grace and Terri rushed into my room and ushered Jemma out.

My sister dug her heels into the floor, but my friends were stronger. "You get away with everything!" she yelled once she'd been successfully booted.

I rolled my eyes. Yeah, that was me, always getting what I wanted. Like a broken heart. Who wouldn't want that? I groaned. Jemma didn't have any clue what my life was like. Terri closed the door behind her, and both she and Grace spoke simultaneously, their voices more anxious than usual.

"Are you okay?" Grace asked.

"You never wrote us back," Terri said.

I tried to smile at them. "I know, I'm sorry. I meant to, but I wasn't thinking straight. And when you said you were coming over, I figured I would explain when you got here."

Grace dropped her bag on the floor and rushed over to me, bending down to give me a giant hug. "It doesn't matter, as long as you're all right."

"Avery's done a good job distracting me," I said, putting up a front as all three of them watched me intently. I could tell they were afraid of how I was going to react. I didn't want to give them more reasons to worry. It wasn't like there was anything they could do to make this better. I just needed to grin and bear it, at least until I was alone. I'd had enough public displays of crying, I didn't need to add to it. "You guys know each other, right?" I asked, changing the subject.

They nodded and exchanged their hellos and then Terri faced me, her hands on her hips à la my sister. "So only Grace gets a hug?"

"I'd never forget you," I said, holding out my hands so she'd come closer.

Terri closed in and whispered in my ear, "We will make him pay."

The words were oddly comforting, but while I loved that she was ready to come to my aid, I didn't want Marc to suffer. I knew I wasn't supposed to feel this way—I was in the middle of a cleansing ritual and all—but what I really wanted was for him to want me back. I kept that little nugget to myself.

Terri squished her way on the bed between where Grace and I were now seated. "Um," she said, picking off a piece of photo that had clung to my shirt. "Why do you have a little Marc head stuck to you? Making voodoo dolls? If so, count me in."

Avery scooped up a pile of little Marc heads. "We have plenty to go around."

My stomach churned again. "We're *ex-orcising* the room of him," I explained.

Grace groaned at my pun. "I wouldn't expect anything else." She turned to look at my wall and let out a whistle. The little Marc shrine by my pillow was gone. I'd hung the pictures back up, though—minus his face. It was a reminder that Marc wasn't in my life anymore. Except that he wasn't entirely gone. There were random shots with him scattered throughout the wall—all of us at Six Flags, me trying to lift him after he won his soccer game, him trying to teach Grace how to ice-skate—and so on. We hadn't gotten to them yet, and I wasn't sure I wanted to. Marc had been a huge part of my life. How was I supposed to just forget him?

"Maybe you should take this whole section down," Grace said, still studying my headless Marc collection. "Put up something that will make you smile."

I shook my head. I needed those photos there. Seeing them made me angry—at him, the situation, everything—and having them gone would only make me sad. Well, sadder.

"I think the new look is brilliant," Terri said and ripped one of the tiny heads into even smaller pieces to emphasize the point. "I can totally get behind this."

I cringed. There was no salvaging that photo now. If I wanted it, I'd need to find it on the cloud. Not that I planned to tape his head back next to mine. Unless, of course, Marc came to his senses. There was still a chance. If he was feeling even the tiniest fraction of what I was feeling, he would come crawling back.

A phone rang. Marc!

I reached for my phone and chided myself when I realized it wasn't mine. Of course it wasn't. Why would I even get my hopes up? He wasn't feeling what I was feeling. He'd brought this on. This was what he *wanted*. I thought for sure I'd cry at the realization, but I didn't. I just felt numb. Maybe the ex-orcism was working.

Avery fumbled with her pocket. "Sorry. It was off, but when someone calls me a few times in a row, it turns itself back on."

I was the last person she needed to apologize to. "You should answer it. It could be important."

Avery shook her head. "It's just Nikki. Nothing to worry about—I saw the texts she sent."

"You sure?" I asked.

"Yeah, she just wanted to know if she should get me a movie ticket."

"Oh my God." I jumped off the bed. "I totally ruined your plans." I looked at Grace and Terri. "All of your plans. I'm so sorry." Grace had a volleyball dinner tonight, and Terri had been planning on going to see some band with a guy she'd met while shopping for paint supplies. Now I felt even worse.

"You didn't ruin anything," Avery said.

In a way she was right. *Marc* did. Yet I was the one keeping them all from going out. I was the one they were stuck with. "Please go have fun. Somebody needs to. It will make me feel better."

No one said anything.

"Please." I put on an extra cheesy smile. "See, I'm doing better already."

Grace and Terri didn't budge, but Avery gnawed at her lip, probably debating if I wanted her to stay or if I needed time alone with my best friends.

I turned my focus to her. "Really. I'm good. You should get out of here."

"If you're sure . . . ," Avery said.

"I am," I answered quickly. I felt guilty enough for having kept her here this long. She didn't need to keep playing babysitter.

"And we're here," Grace joined in, squeezing my arm. "We'll make sure she's okay." I was going to have to deal with getting them out next, but one problem at a time.

"Okay." Avery gave me a little hug. "If you need anything, let me know."

"Unless you can erase tonight from everyone's memories, I'm all set," I said, more to myself than to her. I hated the idea of everyone talking about my breakup.

"People will have your back. You'll see."

I gave a tight-lipped smile this time. I knew the people currently in my room would; I wasn't so sure about anyone else. I had made a fool of myself, and the worst part was that because of my reaction, the whole world was going to know that Marc and I were over. I wasn't ready for that.

"Thanks for being there for me," I said, a lump rising in my throat. So much for being numb to everything. "I don't even know what to say. The way you—"

Avery stopped me. "I told you, we girls have to stick together." Then she waved and headed out.

Once we heard the outside door shut, I dropped back onto my bed and swallowed the urge to cry. "You guys were right. You told me Avery and her group were nice. I guess I'm judgy and awful. No wonder Marc didn't want me. I'm not worth—"

"Hey," Terri said. "Knock it off."

"Yeah," Grace agreed. "Marc's an idiot for not wanting you. It's his loss."

I couldn't talk about this. Not yet. "You guys should get going, too," I said.

"Not happening," Terri said. "How about we finish the Marc purge, huh?"

I was afraid to speak. I was choked up, so I just nodded.

Grace put her hand over mine. "Maybe we should start with this?" she asked softly.

I sucked in some air. I had been clutching my charm bracelet. Playing with it had become second nature over the years. I caught myself doing it all the time. Right now I'd been unwittingly hanging on to a heart-shaped charm with I LOVE YOU engraved on it. The bracelet, with that charm, was the first gift Marc had given me. Each holiday, birthday, special event, he added to it. There was the small cupcake charm for my sweet sixteen, a little peridot for our first anniversary, and a garnet for our second. He even gave me a pearl charm before I left for the summer because I'd be missing our Fourth of July anniversary. I reached for the clasp. Wearing it didn't make sense anymore, but my fingers shook as I tried to take it off. I couldn't do it.

"Here, I got it." Grace went to remove it, but I pulled away.

"No." My voice cracked. Suddenly, those tears I'd been doing such a great job containing came pouring out.

I covered my head with my hands. "How could he do this? What am I going to do?" I sobbed.

Their arms wrapped around me.

I only heard snippets. "We're here." "We love you." "It'll be okay." All of it swirled together. Eventually my cries subdued, but I knew it was only moments before another wave of tears would surface.

Terri stood up and grabbed my computer. "How about a movie? We'll even let you pick. We can get some ice cream and eat it from the carton. It will be like Rom-Com 101."

"Yeah," Grace said. "Your rom-coms are practically how-to guides for you anyway, and this totally fits the bill. The main character always goes through something crappy, deals with a horrible guy, but then finds the real deal—true love and a happily-ever-after. Perfect, right?"

I shook my head. I didn't want to be some character in a movie or book. I wanted to be me in my old life. My regular, same-old, same-old life where my boyfriend, who wasn't horrible—at least not until today—still wanted me. "You guys, I think I just need to be alone."

"No way," Terri objected as Grace shook her head furiously.

"Please," I said.

"But—" Grace started.

"I just want to go to bed, and I can't with both of you watching me. I'll call if I need anything. I promise. Please," I repeated. "I just need some time."

Eventually they conceded, and I was left alone with my thoughts. I felt hollow, but somehow the tears kept coming.

"Cam," my sister said, stepping into my room.

I couldn't take any of her snide comments, not now. "What?"

"I, um, heard you guys."

How many times had I told her not to listen at my door? "Well, now you know," I grumbled through my tears. "Marc dumped me. Happy?"

Jemma moved closer to me. "No. I'm . . ." She watched me, her eyes welling up, too. Then she climbed into my bed and snuggled next to me. "He's dead to me, too," she whispered.

I fell asleep crying into her hair.

Chapter 7

I let out three exaggerated coughs as I entered the kitchen Monday morning.

"Don't even try it," my mother said.

"Try what? I'm sick. I think I need to stay home today."

"You're going to school," she said matter-of-factly, putting a plate of chocolate chip pancakes down on the counter.

I knew she was going to say that. My parents had basically let me stay comatose all weekend, with the caveat that come Monday morning, I'd snap out of it. Easier said than done.

I sat down on the stool in front of the pancakes and stuck my fork into them. I couldn't eat. Every time I swallowed something, I felt like it was going to come back up.

"Hey, kiddo," my dad said, meandering into the kitchen. He shuffled his hand through my tangled mess of hair. "Feeling any better?" My sister trailed after him.

We were not typically morning people. With the exception of a few grunts and nods in the hallway, we barely acknowledged one another at this hour. Everyone was always rushing to do their own thing, but today my mom had called everyone down for breakfast—as if food with my family would make me forget about my problems.

"Actually," I said, holding on to my stomach and groaning, "I think I'm coming down with something."

"Now it's a stomach bug? Thought you had a cough," my mom said, smirking, even though I did not find the circumstances amusing in the least.

"You can have more than one symptom," I informed her.

"You're a sucky faker," my sister said, stealing a pancake off my plate and shoving it in her mouth.

"Because maybe I haven't had as much practice as you," I shot back, smacking her hand away before she could take another. If she wasn't going to come to my aid, then she couldn't eat my breakfast.

It was no secret that my sister had pretended to be ill to get out of school on more than one occasion, yet my parents didn't give *her* a hard time. "You always let Jemma stay home."

"Jemma wasn't trying to ruin her perfect attendance record because of some boy," my mother said, putting a plate of pancakes down for my sister.

Great, so I was being punished because I'd never bothered to pretend I was sick in the past?

"He's not *some* boy." I tossed my fork down. "And it's not like it matters where I get into school now anyway," I muttered.

"Hey," my mom said, leaning over the kitchen counter and putting her hands on my shoulders, "I don't want to hear you talking like this. Your dreams are *your* dreams. Not Marc's."

His name alone brought me to the verge of tears. How was I supposed to go to school like this?

"Come on," my dad said, jumping into the morning pep talk. "Don't you want to show Marc that you're doing fine without him?"

"In that case, she might want to shower," my sister said, scrunching up her nose and dramatically waving her hand in front of it.

I sneered at her.

"What?" Jemma asked, shoving a huge bite of pancake into her mouth. "I'm just trying to help. You're kind of stinking up the place."

I couldn't really argue with her. She was right. I was a mess. A smelly, disgusting one. I was still in the tank top I'd worn to school on Friday and to Scobell's. While I had managed to change out of my jeans and into a pair of gym shorts, I hadn't touched my hair, or bathed, or even put on deodorant. I'd only brushed my teeth because Jemma had brought my toothbrush, toothpaste, and a cup of water into my bedroom and threatened to brush them for me. "Let Marc see what a mess I am, what he did to me. I don't care," I informed them.

"Cammy," my dad said. He hadn't called me that since I was a child. "*We* care, and this isn't healthy."

Neither was having your heart ripped to shreds.

My mother nodded in agreement. "We hate seeing you like this." She was watching me with so much intensity, I had to turn away.

"I look how I feel."

"Then you need to fake it till you make it," she said.

Sometimes my mother could be like a walking meme. I picked my fork back up and stabbed it into my food. "What kind of advice is that?"

"The kind that works," my father said. "When I got my first advertising job, I didn't feel ready, but I pretended I was. I walked the walk, and now look—creative director. Your mom did the same thing."

Did they really not see that this was entirely different from not being prepared for a job?

"It's only been a couple of days," I tried to explain. "You don't get over something like this overnight."

"And you don't get over it by sitting home and sulking," my dad said. "Cammy, we know how hard this is for you, but you need to be strong."

"Your friends will be here soon. Why don't you go get ready?" my mom said, putting on her "soothing" voice. I'd heard it a lot this weekend. I knew she was trying to help, they all were, but it wasn't working.

"I am ready."

"Camryn," my dad said, switching back to my "grown-up" name and his serious voice. "You can't go to school like that."

I wanted to object, but I was too tired to argue anymore, so I bit my tongue and trudged back upstairs.

My phone buzzed. It was Terri.

TERRI
We'll be there in twenty minutes.

I texted back a thumbs-up. There was no use telling *her* no, either; she was almost as bad as my family. Terri was on a mission to cheer me up. Both she and Grace had stopped by on Saturday and Sunday even though I'd told them not to, and I barely spoke to either of them. During the first visit, they put on an old movie. It was *Sleepless in Seattle*, and it used to be one of my favorites, but when the lead left her perfectly lovely fiancé to go find someone else, I burst into tears. Marc was Meg Ryan, and I was the fiancé—some random side character that no one cared about, because they were all rooting for the lead to find someone better. I didn't want to be the throwaway character. I wanted to be the one who found love.

After the movie fiasco, my friends just sat with me while I sulked.

Now they were on their way to pick me up. By pure habit I showered, dressed, and was back downstairs by the time Terri beeped the horn. There was no getting out of it: I was going to school. I took one last look in the mirror, realizing I looked like a ghost version of myself. My hazel eyes, the same color as Marc's, were dull and red-rimmed from all the crying.

I sighed. I so looked the part of the tragically dumped girlfriend. Well, I figured, I might as well fully embrace the role. I rummaged through the junk drawer at the end table by the door and found my giant, round sunglasses. I grabbed a baseball hat off the coatrack, too. I put them both on, my new shields from the world. "Bye!" I shouted to my family as the screen door slammed behind me, not giving them time for one last pep talk.

"Hey!" Grace jumped out of the passenger side and gave me a hug. "You can have shotgun." They never gave me the front. Last one picked up always got the back. They were taking pity on me, but I was not going to object. I'd take any perks I could get.

I got inside and slunk down in the seat. Terri gave my outfit a once-over.

"I call it miserable chic," I told her.

"Hmm," she said. "I think it has more of the famous-actor-trying-too-hard-not-to-get-noticed vibe."

A small smile tugged at my lips, but I pushed it away.

Terri caught me. "No way," she said, shaking her head. "You are not sulking all day. I'm not letting you."

"But I'm so good at it," I moaned.

She laughed. "We know."

Grace reached out and squeezed my shoulder. "You're going to see, the day will be a lot easier than you think."

I threw my head back. "Are we taking bets on that? Because I could use some extra cash."

Terri side-eyed me as she started the car.

"Okay, fine." I gave in begrudgingly. "I'll try to be cheery." Fake it till you make it, that was what my mom had said, and I supposed she had a point.

"Ready?" Terri asked when we pulled into the parking lot at school.

I nodded. "Let's do it."

My confidence waned as I got out of the car and saw so many students lingering outside. I made a sprint toward the building, my friends speed-walking to keep up with me.

"Trying out for the track team?" Terri asked, but I ignored her. My focus was on getting to my locker without anyone stopping me to chat.

We passed a few people in the halls, and I felt them looking in my direction, but the sunglasses were great at keeping accidental eye contact at bay. I wasn't ready to make small talk with anyone. I successfully made it to my destination. Even better, I did it without a single Marc sighting. My goal for today was to avoid him at all costs. There was no way I'd be able to fake anything around him.

"Aren't you going to take those off?" Grace asked, tapping her temple to signal she meant my sunglasses.

"Nope," I said, adjusting the nosepiece. "They and I are one."

Terri's mouth quirked into a smile. "Hey, you be as extra as you need. I, for one, support it fully."

Normally she busted me hard-core when I went what she called "over the top," but today she was encouraging the dramatics. That meant she knew this day was going to be torture. We all did.

The bell rang and a bunch of people ran by. It wasn't an exaggeration to say everyone stared as they passed me. My appearance brought no fewer than five conversations to a halt. Not that I was surprised. Videos of my breakup had been all over social media sites like GroupIt. They'd been taken down, most of them anyway, but not before getting hundreds of views—including about sixty from me. I couldn't help it: I just kept playing the video over and over until my tears blurred out the screen. Then I'd start over.

Despite the gawking, people seemed to be giving me my space. That is, until a couple of random freshmen I'd never spoken to headed my way. They had a look in their eyes that sent a warning signal straight to my gut: It said I was in the presence of pond scum.

"Did you see the video of her?" Guy Number One taunted as he neared, making sure to slow his pace so he could get a good look at me. "So pathetic. Now look at her, trying to get more attention with the whole *woe is me* act. No wonder he dumped her." He didn't care that I could hear him. In fact, it seemed like that was his intent. Then he kept walking, as if he hadn't just insulted a complete stranger.

My muscles tightened, but while I froze, Terri moved into action. "Not so fast," she said, following them, her hands balled into fists. They stopped, and she moved closer until she was only a few inches from them. If I were those guys, I'd have been running. Terri could be scary when she wanted to be.

"What was that you were you saying?" she asked, her voice soft, a low growl designed to send shivers down one's spine. "Care to say it to my face?"

One of them opened his mouth, but when he took in Terri's death glare, complete with raised eyebrow and eyes flashing pure hatred, he snapped it back shut.

"That's what I thought. You want to talk pathetic, try two little freshmen thinking they're big shots. Think of this as your warning to watch yourselves, because next time I won't be so nice."

They scurried off like rats without saying anything else. Smart on their part. I wasn't sure exactly what Terri would have done if they hadn't listened, but knowing her, it would have stung.

"Whoa," Luke, the missing member of our group, said, catching the tail end of things. "What's going on here?" He looked from us to where Terri was still facing down the hall, even though the freshmen were long gone.

"We go to school with assholes," she answered, swiping her hands together as if she were brushing away their memory.

He put his thumbs in his pockets. "Ah, they brought up the break—"

Terri shot him a look, not quite her death one, but close.

"The—the winter break," he stammered, trying to cover. Even though there wasn't a point. I'd already heard him. "You know, underclassmen always complain that once, um, winter break comes, seniors get to slack off. They'll get it when they're in our shoes. Right?"

Luke gave me a meek smile. He was trying so hard. They all were. "Yeah, sure," I said, throwing him a bone, even though we both knew his attempt at a save was pointless.

The bell rang, and I'd never been more relieved and terrified at the same time.

"It'll be okay," Terri said. "I'll be with you first period."

I knew her words were supposed to make me relax, but they didn't. I had a whole day to get through.

"You've got this," Grace whispered.

I flung my backpack over my shoulder. I wished that were true.

Chapter 8

"**W**ait," I told Terri before we stepped out of first period. Everyone else had already filed out, but I wasn't taking any chances. I popped my head through the door and looked in both directions. There was no sign of Marc. "Coast is clear."

I took her arm and pulled her into the hall. We made it about twenty feet when I thought I saw you-know-who. I twirled around and pretended to study a locker. About a minute later, I peered over the top of my sunglasses at the guy who had just passed. "False alarm," I told Terri. "Marc has a shirt like that."

She raised an eyebrow at me, but I ignored the look.

"Remember how I said be as extra as you want?" Terri pressed as we continued down the hall, me scanning the way in case I needed to make a quick dash into a classroom.

She didn't wait for me to answer. "You may want to dial it back. Forget actress in hiding; you look like you're in some bad teen spy movie, or turning into Inspector Gadget or something. All you need is the trench coat."

Both of us had watched more than our fair share of the bumbling cartoon inspector when we babysat the Griffins. "I think I'm a lot cuter than Inspector Gadget."

Terri gave me a look that said I knew what she meant.

"Inspector Gadget always wins in the end—that's something, right?" I said in a lame attempt to lighten the mood and make her stop giving me that face.

She just sighed as we reached her classroom. "Are you going to be okay?"

I nodded, but she looked skeptical.

I hated that I was bringing everyone down and making them all worry about me. So I lowered my sunglasses, winked at her, and pointed my arm down the hall. "Go, go, Gadget is off to conquer the world."

That finally got a laugh out of her. I wasn't sure if it got her to believe I was A-okay, but I decided to quit while I was ahead. I took off for my class, fake smile and all.

I made it through about half the day unscathed, not one little sighting of my ex, but then I hit an obstacle. Lunch.

Before today, I'd never thought twice about where to sit in the cafeteria. This year, my seat was at the big table right in the middle of the room: the soccer table. *Marc's* table. I obviously couldn't go there now. I stood with my tray, carefully positioning myself behind a pillar so that I was out of my ex's line of vision and could survey the area. Grace, Terri, even Luke, all had different lunch periods from me. I wasn't sure where to go, but I couldn't very well keep standing around like a sad statue. Where was I supposed to sit? I didn't want to wind up eating in the bathroom or hiding in some classroom. I did not want to be *that* cliché. Still, it seemed better than having Marc and his friends see me with nowhere to go. My luck and fabulous avoidance skills were about to run out. Marc was bound to notice me in the cafeteria.

When we'd gotten our schedules this summer, I'd been so relieved that we had this period together. Now it seemed like a cruel twist of fate. I ventured a glance at his table. He was laughing. *Laughing!*

How could he be so at ease and happy, while I was struggling to get through the day?

I quickly moved my head back, but I wasn't sure if I was fast enough. Marc looked in my direction. Had he seen me staring? I cursed my second-period teacher for confiscating my hat and sunglasses after I refused to take them off. They really would have come in handy about now. I did not want my puffy eyes on full display. As much as I hated to admit it, my parents were right. I didn't want Marc to know what a train wreck he'd turned me into. I was *not* going to stay hidden. Not for some jerk. I gripped my tray so hard my knuckles turned white, and I took a step out from behind the pillar. I headed toward the back of the room, to nowhere in particular, but I did so with my head held high. I had no clue what I'd do when I reached the wall, but I kept going. Maybe I'd turn around and walk in the other direction? Sit at a random table? Curl up into a ball and pretend I wasn't there? None of these seemed like decent options, but they beat standing around so people could throw me pitying gazes.

"Cam! Cam!"

I wasn't sure where the voice was coming from.

"Cam, over here!" About two tables diagonally from Marc was Avery. She was standing and waving her arms at me.

For the first time all day, I smiled a *real* smile.

"Hey," I said, relief washing over me as I made my way to her and dropped my tray in front of an empty stool.

"Hi." As I started to sit, Avery put up a finger. "You should switch seats with Nikki."

"Why?" Nikki asked.

Avery ever so subtly moved her eyes from our table to Marc's, but I caught it. From the seat I was about to take, I'd have a full view of my ex. If I sat in Nikki's seat, my back would be to him.

"Ohhh," Nikki said, sliding out of her spot and moving around the table until she was next to Avery. "Right. Take my seat. You do *not* need to look at that all period."

"Nikki, stop . . . ," Avery hissed.

"Sorry, but come on, isn't it weirder if we don't talk about it at all?" She turned to me. "I mean, I was at the diner, and it's not a secret that the video was just about everywhere. At least until Avery made those—"

"Nikki!" Avery snapped again.

"Wait, what?" I plunked down in the seat. "You had it taken down?"

Avery shrugged.

When it became obvious she wasn't going to say anything more, Nikki answered for her. "Oh my God, you should have seen her. She was texting like a madwoman when she got to the movie theater. And when Olena Richardson refused to remove the video, Avery wasn't having it. She kindly reminded Olena of a few pictures from her birthday party that the Richardsons would flip out about. Little Miss Perfect Olena was not acting so perfect. Not even sixty seconds later, the video was gone from her page."

"You did that for me?" I'd noticed the videos had disappeared, but I hadn't really thought about how or why.

Avery shrugged again. "It wasn't a big deal."

It was to me.

"What's a little blackmail among friends," Nikki joked.

"It wasn't blackmail," Avery corrected, her eyes twinkling.

"Not quite. I simply helped her come to her senses. Cam said she wanted to make what happened disappear. I figured I could at least try."

When I'd said that, I hadn't meant for her to take me seriously, but I was grateful she had. "Thank you," I told her. "Really."

"Anyway," Avery said, changing the subject, "do you know everyone?" She pointed next to her. "The blabbermouth here is Nikki; you'll get used to her."

"Very funny," Nikki said. "She'll love me—everyone does." I wasn't sure if she was joking or not, but it made me laugh either way.

Avery threw a chip at her. "Don't mind her modesty."

"Modesty is overrated," Nikki answered, and ate the chip to accentuate her point.

"Uh-huh," Avery said, humoring her, before introducing the other two girls at the table—Meg and Naamua. They were all on the cheerleading team.

"Thanks for letting me sit with you guys," I told them. I resisted the urge to turn around and check out Marc's table, but I couldn't help but wonder if he was watching me. Did he want to know how I was doing? Did he feel any remorse at all?

"So?" Nikki asked.

"What?" I had spaced out. Had she asked me something?

"There is one thing I want to know," Nikki continued.

Was this going to be a whole rehash of my life with Marc? I didn't want to talk about him, I didn't even want to say his name, but I couldn't just get up and leave. I'd just sat down.

Avery elbowed Nikki, but it didn't stop her. "What I'm dying to know," Nikki said after a long dramatic pause, "is how you eat these school lunches. They're gross." She made a gagging expression at my

lunch, and just like that the subject changed from my public humiliation and Avery's heroism to the merits of the so-called sloppy joes
the cafeteria served up. For a full twenty minutes, I didn't have to
think or talk about Marc.

I finally felt like I could breathe again.

Chapter 9

My Marc respite continued until last period. I dragged my feet from physics to art class. This was it. This was where I was going to be face-to-face—or rather side-by-side—with Marc. Our easels were right next to each other. This was the class I'd fought for so I could be near him. Life was cruel. Not only would it probably put my perfect GPA in jeopardy, but it was going to make me work beside my ex on a project I had zero interest in. Knowing Marc, he'd try to make small talk, see if we could be "friends." Who would have thought such a nice little word could feel like knives cutting into my skin?

I had to stop stalling. I was going to be late. This was ridiculous. *I* was being ridiculous. I marched up to the classroom. This wasn't a big deal. I could do it—I just needed to go inside, get my supplies, and try to focus on my painting. Yet somehow I couldn't get my feet to move. Marc was standing just fifteen feet away. His back was to me, but he still made my stomach perform an acrobatic act. I wasn't sure if it was because I didn't want to be near him—or because I did. I wasn't supposed to still want Marc, my brain knew that, but my heart was having a harder time getting the message. I hovered by the door, watching him. He was tying his smock around his waist and talking to Todd. They were both so relaxed. It wasn't fair. I was supposed to be in there joking around with them, smiling, making fun of our art projects, planning our senior year. Instead the warning bell was sounding, and I was glued to the floor just outside our classroom, gaping at them.

Todd caught me staring.

Just perfect. I gave him a smile, hoping it came off less forced than it felt. Just because Marc and I were over, it didn't mean things had to be weird with Todd. He was my friend, too. Over the years, I'd hung out with him almost as much as I'd hung out with Grace and Terri.

He nudged Marc's side. "Looks like someone has a stalker."

I felt a lump rise in my throat. Why was Todd making fun of me? I stared at him in disbelief, but I shouldn't have given him the satisfaction. From the look on his face, he was enjoying my reaction. I'd always thought he liked me. Had he just been humoring me all these years for Marc's sake?

He snorted and slapped the back of his hand on Marc's chest. "Man, you totally traded up."

Marc laughed nervously.

Really? He wasn't defending me. The guy I'd been dating for forever had not only dumped me publicly but was now joining in on crap talk about me? Before I knew it, I was standing inches away from him. My thoughts were flying.

"Seriously. *Seriously?*" I asked.

He turned around.

I didn't give him a chance to speak. "I've cheered you on for how many of your stupid soccer games, quizzed you on SAT words for way longer than is humanly necessary, babysat your brother when your parents were away so you wouldn't miss practice, and this is how you talk about me?"

"Um—it's—" he stammered, his focus shifting to my wrist.

Shoot. I was playing with the bracelet again, and he'd noticed. I knew I should have gotten rid of the thing, or at least taken it off, but I felt naked without it, and I was already having a tough enough week.

"I'm—" he continued, but I cut him off. I didn't want to hear it.

"Yeah, I know," I said, *"you traded up."*

Then the meaning of the words hit me. Marc was already dating. It was hard to breathe. He was really doing it, going out with other people. Experiencing all the "fun" he'd missed out on because he'd been stuck with me. I didn't know what to do.

I fumbled with my wrist until I got the clasp of the charm bracelet undone. It felt like it was searing my skin. I took it off and threw the thing at him. Then I turned on my heels and made a beeline out of the classroom and straight for the exit.

I was *so* done with this day.

Chapter 10

Somehow I made it to my house, even though the whole walk home felt like a blur. Marc was really moving on. How was this real? I just needed to lock myself away in my room with a gallon of macaroni and cheese and my favorite rom-coms and live in the world of happily-ever-afters.

I unlocked the door, trying hard to ignore the sight of my naked wrist. The charms from my bracelet always jingled when I turned the doorknob. Now there was an aching silence. Momentarily, anyway.

"Cam!" my mom shouted, slapping her hand over her chest in surprise as I walked into the house.

I jumped back. "Mom!" I'd made it out of school without anyone noticing just to be caught by my mother? When was my luck going to turn around? "What are you doing here this early?"

"I had a meeting nearby, but I think the real question is what are *you* doing here now?"

My mind raced for a good excuse. "Early dismissal?"

"Are you asking me or telling me?"

I debated digging deeper into the lie, but my mom had a way of getting to the truth. I decided to fess up early. Maybe it would mean she wouldn't ground me. Not that I really cared; it wasn't like I had anywhere I wanted to go.

I went to the living room and flung myself on the couch and told her about art class.

She frowned. "So you cut last period? Cam . . ."

I hated when she used that disappointed tone of voice.

"I couldn't stay there, and come on," I said, "I deserve this. I've never skipped. Not once. So missing one class in my senior year is not a big deal."

"It is when you're doing it to avoid someone."

I sat up. "Mom, you don't get it. Seeing him . . . him saying . . . forget it . . . you wouldn't understand."

She sat down next to me and rubbed my back. "Of course I understand. I've had my share of heartbreaks."

"Right," I said with an extra dose of sarcasm. I'd heard the stories. My dad always talked about how my mom was a "heart-breaker." She was the one who'd always done the dumping, not the one left crying. "Not the way Dad tells it."

"Your dad left out some parts." My parents knew each other in high school, but they didn't get together until their tenth reunion. "Like my college years."

I rolled my eyes. She'd had a long-term boyfriend then, too. She'd called it off when she graduated or something like that. "Yeah, I'm sure it was really hard for you to break someone's heart. Boo-hoo."

I didn't care if that was cold. At the moment I felt more sympathy for the dumpee, not the dumper.

"Calling things off with someone you care about, someone you may even love, is not easy, either," she said.

I jumped up. "You're seriously going to talk to me about that now? You want me to feel bad for Marc? Great pep talk, Mom."

"You didn't let me finish," she said, taking my hands in hers and guiding me back down to the seat cushion. "Yes, I hurt people, unintentionally, but you can't stay with someone because you don't want to hurt their feelings. It's not good for either of you." She *really* sucked at this. Did she want to make me cry again? Where were the happy little slogans she was always spouting? Even those were better than this. Before I could say anything, she continued. "*But* I've been in your shoes, too."

I waited for her to continue.

"Freshman year at Penn, I was lab partners with my ex-boyfriend. An ex who had been sneaking around with my roommate. When I found out, I still had to work with him for another two months and continue living with my roommate. I couldn't even escape to my room to get away from it all."

My eyes bulged and my mouth practically fell to the floor. "What? How have I never heard *this* story before?"

She squeezed my hands. "Because it was a long time ago. A footnote in my story. It doesn't define me. If anything, it made me stronger."

I wasn't sure how to respond. It sounded like torture, even worse than what I was going through now. "How did you deal?"

"One day at a time. I vowed not to let them ruin my college experience. I went out, I did things—even when I didn't want to. I hung out with my friends, made some new ones, and started dating again. Pretty soon, it became one of those funny roommate horror stories, something to laugh about instead of cry over. Cam, you can't control how people treat you, but you can control how you react to it. If I could get through that, you can get through this. It's your senior year; you're supposed to enjoy it."

"Not everyone does," I reminded her.

"You're not everyone. You're my daughter. You're smart, beautiful, stubborn as hell, larger than life, and all-around amazing. If Marc can't see that, then you don't want him. But don't let him take this year from you. You, my love, deserve everything your heart desires, so go out and get it."

I stood up. "I'll think about it."

"Don't think about it," she said. "Just do it."

I groaned. That was all well and good for a Nike ad, but just because I wanted to feel nothing for Marc didn't mean I knew how to make that a reality.

She stood up and kissed the top of my head. "You got this."

I nodded.

"And Cam," she said, "no skipping tomorrow. You're going to that class."

I threw my head back. "Can't you just ground me? Make me stay home?"

"No such luck."

"Fine, whatever," I said, heading into the kitchen. I really needed that mac and cheese now.

I raided the fridge for my food supplies and went to my room for some rom-com therapy.

As I was scrolling through my movies on my laptop, FaceTime popped up. It was Terri. Grace's face was squished up against hers, with Luke's hovering above so that they could all fit on the screen.

"Where are you?" Grace asked.

My mouth was filled with cheesy goodness, so I just gestured around me at the room.

Terri moved in closer to the camera until she was the only person I was able to see. "We came to meet you after class, so imagine our surprise when we found out you left."

I put my bowl on the nightstand. I was losing my appetite. I knew my friends were just trying to be there for me. It was super sweet that they wanted to make sure my Marc class had been okay, but it was another reminder of everything that had gone wrong.

"Spill it," Terri said. "What happened?"

She moved back so the others could see me, too.

I knew they'd get it out of me eventually, so after making sure they were out of earshot of anyone wandering the halls of Brooksvale High, I gave them the gory details of art class and finding out that Marc was apparently already dating.

"I'm sorry, Cam," Grace said.

I let out a long breath.

"Hey, don't get upset," Luke added. "So he's going on a few dates, it's not like it means anything."

Maybe that was true, and there was a chance that after Marc went out with a couple of different people, he'd realize he was meant to be with me.

Terri glared at Luke and then turned her attention back to the phone. "Ignore him. Cam, I know what you're thinking," Terri said, "and you need to stop. Marc sucks. You don't want him back."

"But he was the *one*."

"Nooo!" Terri growled. "He was not 'the one,' and you've got to stop with that stuff. It's not going to help. Besides, in case you've forgotten, we're in *high school*. Who needs that now?"

"But—"

She cut me off, her finger aimed straight at me through her phone. "I will literally scream if you start talking about anagrams."

I wasn't going to, although it was a pretty good guess. I may have on *a few* (give or take a hundred) occasions mentioned how cute it was that the letters in *Cam* made up most of the letters in *Marc*. I thought it was fate.

I looked to Grace for some backup, for a sign of hope that Marc and I were meant to be, but I didn't get any. She was biting her lip, which meant she didn't want to tell me what she really thought.

"How about some company?" she said instead. "I can come over after practice."

"You have your thing," Terri reminded her.

"What thing?" I asked.

Grace shook her head. "It's nothing. I was just supposed to hang out with Derrick."

I sat up straighter. "You guys have a second date?" She had sent me hundreds of texts about him over the summer, and he'd finally asked her out right before break ended.

"Third, actually."

"Wait, what?" I practically dropped my computer. "Why didn't you tell me?"

She bit her lip. "Because it's not a big deal."

"Uh, yeah, it is. It means you saw Derrick this weekend and didn't say anything." I had been such a bad friend, moping and worrying about my own problems, that I hadn't even known Grace was seeing someone or what Terri had been up to. I needed to be better. This was huge news. Grace hung out with people here and there, but she hadn't really dated anyone since freshman year, and this sounded like it had real potential. "You are not canceling because of me. You are going on that date, and I want details."

"All right, all right." She laughed, her eyes lighting up. "I hate to do this, but I have to get to practice."

"Go," I said. "I'm fine."

"I'll call you later," she said, and waved goodbye.

"Luke and I can still come over," Terri said, taking back over the conversation.

"You both have better things to do than babysit me," I told her.

Terri shrugged her shoulder. "Me, maybe. Him? Probably not."

Luke pretended to stab a dagger into his chest and shook his head at Terri. "I don't know why I hang out with you."

"Because you love me," she joked.

He winked at her. "You should be so lucky."

It made me queasy how they could joke about love and feelings. They'd gone out on dates. They'd kissed. And now they were just friends. Yeah, it had been years ago . . . but it made me think of Marc. He and I were never going to get to that place. I didn't want us to—I wanted more.

"I don't need company," I told them.

"It will be fun," Terri said, focusing her attention back on me.

"Not for you. I'm going to be watching rom-coms."

"I can suffer through."

I grabbed my bowl of mac and cheese. "I'm fine. Honest."

Terri sucked in her cheeks and studied my face. She moved down the hall, so it was just me and her. No more Luke. "You sure?" she asked, her voice low. "We can hang out, just you and me."

After assuring her a dozen more times that I was all right, she gave in.

"Okay, I'll leave you with your movies, *but*," she said, emphasizing the word, "you have to promise you won't watch one where the girl gets back with her crappy ex."

"No promises," I said, loading up my fork with another giant heap of macaroni. "I love second-chance romances."

She shook her head. "Uh-uh, it will give you too many ideas. Contrary to your life motto, life isn't a rom-com. Promise me you'll pick something else to watch."

I wanted to argue the merits of living life as a romantic comedy, but I didn't have it in me. Right now, my life was anything but romantic. Instead I just agreed with her. "All right. I promise."

We said our goodbyes, and I resumed scrolling through my movie choices. Between the streaming networks and all the movies I bought, I had quite the impressive selection. Even if I ignored all the second-chance romances, there were tons of other tropes to choose from. Friends to lovers, secret romance, falling for a royal, pretend relationships . . .

I gasped.

The last one caused the tiniest sliver of an idea to form.

A bad idea. A *really* bad idea.

An idea Terri would positively hate, but an idea that could be my answer to everything. An idea that kept growing and growing and was now going full steam throughout my head and taking over my entire being.

What if I really did try to live in a rom-com? Date someone else to make my ex jealous, and maybe, possibly, hopefully, fall for the new guy. I'd watched it happen on-screen and read it in books hundreds of times.

Or, at the very least, maybe I'd rile up Marc so much, he'd come running back. This could work. Yeah, Terri was going to kill me, but it was worth a try.

I deserved the senior year I'd dreamed about.

I was going to find someone so much better than Marc and rub his face in it. I was going to get into Columbia and live my dream New York life. I was going to get my happily-ever-after. I might even find love.

But most of all, I was going to make Marc regret dumping me.

Chapter 11

My alarm blared Tuesday morning. For once there was no snoozing, no pulling the covers over my head, no wishing it were still the weekend. I was ready to go back to school. I was on a mission—to find a new boyfriend, to get into Columbia, and to have an amazing senior year. My plan to make it all happen was going into motion today. Thoughts swirled in my head as I showered and got ready. I could do this. Who needed Marc? I tossed on a fitted black turtleneck and a pair of black pants, and I pulled my hair back into a tight bun. This was my cool, collected, *don't mess with me, I've got this*, New Yorker look, or at least my interpretation of it based on what I had in my closet.

"Why do I get the impression you're about to unveil a new iPhone on me?" my dad asked, looking up from his cup of coffee when I entered the kitchen.

"What?" I asked.

"It's what Steve Jobs wore when—" He waved his free hand. "Forget it. Doesn't matter. I'm just glad to see you smiling."

I hadn't even realized I was, although it didn't last long. Jemma stopped rifling through the refrigerator long enough to give me a once-over. "I think she looks more like a mime . . . or a sad excuse for a ninja."

My sister quickly turned any grin I'd been sporting into a scowl. "A ninja who can kick your—"

"All right, enough of that," my mom said, joining us in the kitchen. "But I am glad to see you're getting back to your old self." She kissed the top of my head.

"Better than ever." I knew that was the type of corny thing you said to appease your parents and make them think everything was all right, but in this instance I actually meant it. I was ready for the next part of my life to start.

I grabbed a sip of my dad's coffee and a cereal bar, then yelled my goodbyes to my family as Terri honked her horn. Both she and Grace were leaning against the car, fake smiles barely masking their concern, as they watched me approach.

"Were you afraid you'd need to coax me inside?" I asked. Normally, they didn't get out of the car to meet me. If anything, one of them would shove their head through the window and yell at me to hurry up.

"We're just worried," Grace said.

"I know, but I told you, you don't need to be. I'm good. Really good. In fact"—I wiggled my eyebrows at them—"I have a plan that's going to turn my year around."

They looked at each other, and I could feel the skepticism oozing off them.

"Hey," I protested. "You haven't even heard it yet."

Terri gestured for me to continue.

"I'm finding someone new. It's like that saying: The best way to get over an old guy is to find a new one."

Terri smirked. "That's not quite how it goes . . ."

"Cam . . . ," Grace said, and bit her lip. "Don't you want to wait a little? Give yourself some time?"

"Time for what? To meet someone new? Marc didn't need to wait to get over me; I don't need to wait to get over him."

Terri nodded. "You're right. Believe it or not, I actually agree with you."

I was glad I'd left out the part that I also hoped this would make Marc come crawling back to me. I liked having Terri's support. When it came to dating, relationships, and guys, she and I rarely saw eye-to-eye.

"Dating around will do you good," she told me as she walked over to the driver's side of the car and got in. There was an instant shift in her body language. She'd gone from being all worried about me to being a woman with a plan. "You're going to like it, you'll see. I can already think of so many people you'll love. This is going to be fun. I'm going to make sure you have dates for the rest of the year."

I should have known we wouldn't be on the same page. "I don't plan on dating around." I stared at her through the window. "I plan on having *a* boyfriend. One."

She rolled her eyes. "Okay, and just how do you think you'll find this boyfriend? *From dating around.* After which you'll realize relationships are overrated."

I groaned. Just because Marc *might* not be the one didn't mean that I didn't want to find the real thing eventually. I absolutely wanted my OTP—my one true pairing. "I'm not the only one who wants a relationship. Grace does, too. She just had a third date last night—which I still want details on, Miss I-Barely-Texted-Anything-About-My-Evening." I nudged Grace's arm. "Back me up here."

She shrugged her shoulders and looked down at the ground. "I wouldn't . . . Derrick and I. We're . . . it's not serious. It's . . . we're . . . nothing."

"What? What happened?" I asked. "You said the date was fun." That was pretty much all I'd gotten out of her last night.

"It was—it's not that. It's . . . I don't want to get into it." Derrick Walker had seemed perfect for her. I studied her face. It looked like there was something she wasn't saying. A feeling of dread washed over me. "Was this because of me? Did my breakup scare you off? Because I'm still a believer in love. Don't let my mess of a love life influence yours."

"No, no," she assured me. "Nothing like that. Really, it's not worth talking about."

"Are you sure?"

"Positive."

I wanted to ask more, but I didn't want to push. I knew what it was like to just want to be left alone. "Okay," I said, "but I'm here if you want to talk. And you know what? I already came up with a new guy for me; I'll just come up with one for you, too."

"That's okay," Grace said, holding up her hands to slow me down. "I'm fine. I'm busy with volleyball and college applications. I don't need a new guy. Let's focus on your dating life."

"How about we focus on getting in the car," Terri countered, popping her head out her open window. "We're going to be late."

"Fine," I said, and gestured to Grace to take the front seat. I didn't want any more special treatment.

Grace snapped her seat belt shut. "So who is this new guy you have your heart set on?"

"He's perfect. In fact, he was partially inspired by you."

She framed her face with her hands. "You mean you're picking a cute Korean athlete?"

"Well, if I thought your brother was single . . ."

Grace shuddered. "Don't even joke." For years, most of Grace's friends, myself included, had commented on how hot her brother was, but since he was also four years older than us, it really grossed her out. "He's way too old for you, and he's with Melinda."

"Calm down, I'm not going after your brother. Your fury over Lissi was my muse."

Terri eyed me through the rearview mirror. She may have sensed what was coming.

"Huh?" Grace asked.

"I see how annoyed you get with Lissi at volleyball, and I thought, *Who gets under Marc's skin like that?* And I remembered. Brandon Paunovic." Brandon was a junior on the soccer team who got bumped to varsity his freshman year, stealing away Marc's beloved spotlight. How perfect would it be if Brandon stole away my heart, too?

Terri shook her head. "So this all about making Marc jealous? Cam, come on."

"No, it's not like that. It's just an added bonus. I liked one soccer guy, why not another?" I didn't know Brandon too well. Definitely not enough to call him and say hi or anything. He hadn't been one of Marc's close friends, so he wasn't one of mine, but I had the perfect way to get a reintroduction. "This is going to work. Going out with Brandon is even going to help me get into Columbia."

"What are you talking about?" Grace asked as we pulled into the school lot.

"You'll find out soon enough. I texted Luke to meet me before homeroom. I need him for my plan to work."

Terri turned off the car but was still gripping the steering wheel tight. "Please tell me this isn't one of your harebrained *my life is like a sitcom* schemes."

"Maaayyyybeeee," I said, drawing out the word. There was nothing wrong with my schemes; in fact, I was rather fond of them. Especially if they gave Marc a taste of his own medicine. I got out of the car. "There's Luke—come on."

When we approached him, I made sure I was all smiles. "Hi," I said, using my sweetest voice possible.

He'd been leaning against the wall, but stood up straight and crossed his arms over his chest. "Oh no, this can't be good," Luke said.

"It's not," Terri volunteered.

I swatted my hand in front of my face as if shooing away her words. She didn't know my whole plan, but I did, and the more I thought about it, the more I liked the idea.

I gave Luke what I hoped were giant puppy-dog eyes. "I need to write a story for the paper."

"So why are you coming to me?" Luke asked. "I write features; I'm not the editor. I don't assign anything."

"Yeah," I said, batting my eyelashes at him in an over-the-top comical way, not an *I'm actually hitting on you* one, "but you're good friends with the editor—you have pull. You've been on the paper since freshman year and can get my article approved. It'll be good, I promise. And it will help me get back at Marc."

He shook his head at me. "What do you plan on writing? A story about how evil your ex is? They won't publish it."

"No," I said. "In fact, it's the opposite. I want to do it on how fantastic Brandon Paunovic is. Think about it. Junior soccer star who's already being scouted by schools, who makes Marc writhe with jealousy. It will make a great story."

It would also be the perfect in to get to know Brandon.

"So, let me get this straight," Luke said. "You want to use the school paper to meet a guy?"

I shrugged. "Yeah. *But* it would also be something I could add to my applications. You know I need to pump up my extracurriculars. I was going to ask you about maybe writing something anyway. This just combines that with helping my love life. I'm all about multitasking."

Luke groaned, but I was serious.

An article would be another tangible item I could put on my résumé, and if it helped me get a boyfriend and make Marc seethe, all the better.

Grace laughed. "You never cease to amaze me," she said, and I could tell she supported my plan. She had that glint in her eye that said she wanted to see how this played out just as much as I did. Terri, on the other hand, looked more skeptical.

She just didn't understand—she wasn't a big enough rom-com fan to see the merits of my plan. I was creating the perfect scenario. I could picture it now: Brandon and me meeting for the interview, our eyes locking, the instant chemistry, and before you knew it, we'd be a new power couple.

I put my hands in a steeple and shook them in front of Luke. "Come on, please."

He looked to Terri, and I silently pleaded with her. Luke would do what she said; we both knew it.

"She's going to find a way to do it anyway," Terri told him. "You might as well help her."

Luke put his hands over mine. "You win. I'll ask, but no promises."

I jumped up and down in place. "Thank you, thank you, thank you."

This was going to work. *Brandon and Cam. Bram.* I even liked the sound of it. Brandon was perfect boyfriend material. We had potential to be the real deal.

Even better?

It was going to annoy the crap out of Marc.

Chapter 12

When the bell rang for the start of my lunch period, I was seated in the guidance counselor's office, praying that Ms. Vail would see me. I'd told the front desk that it was urgent. Now I was waiting with crossed fingers and toes that she'd agree to a last-minute appointment.

Ms. Vail popped her head out from her office. "Cam? Come on in."

I didn't need to be asked twice.

"Is everything okay?" she asked, moving some papers around on her desk. An open Tupperware filled with salad was on her desk. I was interrupting her lunch. I hoped she wouldn't hold that against me.

I nodded. "I promise this won't take long. I've been thinking a lot about what you said about my college applications. I'm already looking into writing for the paper, and I came up with an idea for something else that I think will really help. It just needs your approval."

She raised an eyebrow, and I continued on with my pitch.

"Well," I said, trying to keep my voice businesslike, "at the end of English class, Ms. Jackson keeps telling everyone she needs volunteers for the yearbook or it's not going to have any candid photos, collage pages, and so on. No one's stepped up to help. I was thinking it could be something for me to take the lead on."

Ms. Vail glanced at her salad. "You don't need my permission to sign up for a club, Cam."

"I know, but I do need you to make it count as a class."

She rubbed her fingers on her temples. "An extracurricular doesn't get you academic credit, and we don't offer a yearbook class."

"But," I interjected, "you do have a last-period Photoshop class with Ms. Jackson. I took it last year, and I was good at it. I know I can't take it again, but I was thinking we could switch me in there and count it as an independent study. Ms. Jackson gets the help she needs, I get something to write on my application, and the senior class gets a yearbook that is more than just the bare minimum." Added bonus, I would get out of that horrible art class with Marc, but I wasn't going to say that—not yet.

"Cam—"

"Before you say no, think about it. There's a class for chorus, and people write that down as an extracurricular. This is no different. Besides, I'll still have to do outside work. A lot of it. No one's signed up for the yearbook, and Ms. Jackson has a whole folder on her computer of photos students emailed that they want included in it. There's no one to go through them, no one to do the layout or the color correction. That could be me. Ms. Jackson is already on board." I pulled out a note and handed it to Ms. Vail. "In fact, she said it would be a huge help."

I had spoken to Ms. Jackson right after English. I knew she'd like the idea. She was the adviser for the yearbook and was practically begging people to sign up. There'd been no takers. This was an answer to her problem—*and* mine.

Ms. Vail finished reading the note and put it down on her desk.

"Cam, I appreciate what you went through to try to make this happen. But this is something you can do on your own time. It simply doesn't qualify for an independent study."

"It should," I said, way too loud. I brought my volume down. "What's the difference between this and my painting a picture in art class? That's all I'd be giving up. And learning how to work with photos actually has career potential for me. It's something I can do and want to improve on." It wasn't something I'd really thought about before, but it wasn't out of the realm of possibilities. "My painting skills are a joke. If there was an advanced Photoshop class, I'd take it, but there isn't one. So this is my chance. I'll be sitting in the back of Ms. Jackson's class working. When I have questions, she'll be able to answer them, just like she does when students work on their projects for her Photoshop class. Please, this is important to me. It's a class I want, but I also need."

"I hear what you're saying," Ms. Vail said, "but first you spent all summer pleading to get into Ms. Winters's art class, and now you want to get out of it? How do I know you won't be coming in here next week asking for something else?"

I could hear the exasperation dripping off her voice.

"I won't. I've never done this before. I never even set foot in this office before this year. I know it seems strange and out of the blue," I continued, "but it's not. I tried painting. I suck at it. Which would be fine, if my future wasn't at stake. In a way, this is all because of you."

She raised her eyebrow at me again.

"You got me thinking about my hobbies and extracurriculars. I take awesome photos. And the ones that aren't, I can make them look great through editing. You told me I need something to help my application. This is it. Ms. Jackson knows her stuff. I'll learn more being in her class and asking questions than I ever would making a painting of dot clusters. The classes are the same period. It won't mess up anything. Please."

Ms. Vail picked up the note from Ms. Jackson again. She looked from it to me before letting out a long exhale.

"Fine," she said. "I'll see what I can do. But this is it. No more changes. Your schedule will be final."

I let out a small shriek of joy. "Got it. No more changes. Not a problem."

In fact, it was the opposite of a problem. It was perfect.

No more art class, no more being trapped in a room with Marc, no more getting stuck in the past. I was making my future happen, and I'd already gotten past the first hurdle.

Chapter 13

It took longer than I'd have liked, but Luke came through. The editor of the *Brooksvale Bulletin* agreed to let me write the article about the up-and-coming soccer star. Brandon seemed pumped about it, and before I knew it, we were emailing and texting back and forth almost every day. It was usually about soccer, but it was a start, and I could work with it.

We planned to meet in person, but our schedules didn't line up at all. We didn't have any classes together, not even study hall or lunch, and between his soccer schedule and his parents' rules about not going out on a school night, meeting in person for any extended amount of time was trickier than I'd hoped.

When we finally found time for a face-to-face, he had already answered all my interview questions electronically, and I had pretty much finished the article.

"This sweater work?" I asked Terri as I twirled around in my bedroom in a red V-neck. It was about the tenth top I'd tried on. It was just her and me. Grace was stuck in a late volleyball practice— the team had been going hard-core since they'd just scraped by to get their last win.

"Yes," Terri said, throwing herself back on my bed amid my pile of previously tried-on clothes. "As did this one and this one and this one." She tossed the shirts into the air as she spoke. Her tone was light and cheery, but she sounded off.

"Hey," I said, "are you okay?"

"Yeah," she answered before letting out a giant sigh. "I guess. It's nothing serious."

I sat down next to her. "What's going on?"

She twisted a T-shirt around her hands. "Looks like I won't be going to art school next year."

"What are you talking about? You're going to have your pick of where to go." Terri was a shoo-in. Her talent was off the charts. "Trust me, RISD and SVA will be going to war over you."

"Good luck to them, because they'll be up against my parents, and I already lost that battle today. Can't imagine they'll do any better."

"What do you mean?"

Terri propped herself up against my wall. "I told you how they finally called me in for one of the guidance-counselor appointments today? Before I came over here, I told my parents about it. It was like we weren't even on the same planet when it came to college. They pretty much vetoed any type of visual arts school. They want me to get a liberal arts degree. They think it will make me more"—she put on a stern face and faked a man's voice—"'well-rounded. If you want to have a focus in art, that's fine; just make sure all of your bases are covered.'" Terri went back to her regular voice. "It makes no sense. It's not like a sociology or art history degree would be so helpful in getting me a career, either."

She shook her head. "They're full of it, too. If I wanted to go to business school, they wouldn't care if I wasn't 'well-rounded.' It's about the art. They think it's a silly little hobby that I'll grow out of. Or at least they hope I will, but it's not going to happen. It's my everything."

"We'll just make them see that," I told her.

She scoffed. "No we won't. My dad is all 'there are lots of good liberal arts colleges here in Connecticut; go to school here' and my mom is all 'I loved BU—I know you would, too.' They don't care what I want." Terri was on the verge of tears. I'd rarely ever seen her cry. This was major.

"Hey," I said, putting my arm around her, "we're going to come up with a plan that will change their minds. I promise. I got you."

Terri wiped her eyes with her arm and then fanned her face with her hand, trying to regain her composure.

"Yeah." She stood up.

I knew she didn't believe that her parents would change their minds, but I did. We were going to figure out a way to sway them. I was sure of it.

"Enough about me and my problems. Don't we have a date to get you ready for?" she asked, clearly trying to change the subject.

"I don't have to do that today," I told her. "I can reschedule. Why don't we do something instead? Grab some pizza, go to your place before my sister gets home and bothers us, and get your mind off things."

"No way." Terri took my hands and pulled me off the bed.

I opened my mouth to protest, but Terri held up her finger.

"You finally found a time to meet up with Brandon. I'm not letting you miss it. Got it?"

"Fine," I conceded as she handed me some earrings to try on.

Then she scrunched up her face. "Wait? Does Brandon actually know this is a date and not just you taking a photo for the article?"

"I think so," I said, holding one of the dangly blue crystal-like earrings up to my ear and studying it in the mirror. "I did say we needed to celebrate 'wrapping up.' He has to know, right?"

Terri took the earring back and handed me some shiny red studs instead. "Not necessarily. Not if you were you and came across all businesslike."

"I was flirty! See for yourself."

I handed her my phone, and she scrolled through my texts, reading a few out loud.

"'It's going to be a great article.' 'You make a very interesting subject.' 'I'll take a great photo of you.' 'Sure, I can do Scobell's on Friday.'"

Her mouth was twitching.

"What?" I asked, watching her face through the mirror.

"It's just—" She broke out laughing. "I can't believe you think that's flirting. 'You make an *interesting* subject.' Cam! Why didn't you come to me? I would have helped you."

I dropped the earring on my nightstand. "I didn't think I needed help. I *thought* I was doing fine." I waved off her laughter. "It'll work out—with his schedule, he wouldn't make time if he wasn't a little curious about getting to know me better. He has to know it's a date—or at least a feeling-each-other-out kind of thing. Whatever. I'm much more relaxed in person. He'll be enchanted. You'll see."

She nodded. "I'm sure it will be very *interesting*."

I tossed one of my discarded shirts at her. "Shut up," I said, laughing. "It's going to be great. He'll go from story subject to boyfriend."

"Very ethical of you," she teased. "Journalism at its finest."

"Ha-ha. It's not affecting how I write the soccer story. Besides, this isn't the *Times*; it's a high school fluff piece. It's expected, practically encouraged. I think my integrity will stay intact. Plus, it makes for *such* a good meet-cute."

"A meet-what?" Terri asked.

"You know," I explained, "a cute way the two leads meet. Bumping into each other, winding up with seats together on an airplane, getting picked to work on a project together, something that brings them together. Something organic, not something forced."

"This is very organic," she mocked.

But Terri could joke all she wanted. This was going be perfect, just like in the movies.

Chapter 14

I smoothed down my skirt as I stood outside Scobell's. It was a few minutes after seven, time for my date, and yet, despite my earlier excitement, I was having a hard time going inside. In all my planning, I'd forgotten how daunting first dates could be. It was hitting me hard now.

A couple of guys who looked vaguely familiar pushed past me to get to the front door. The diner was packed, which I'd expected—it was Friday night—but it made me feel antsy nonetheless.

This was the first time I'd been back to Scobell's since the Marc incident. My parents had even let me borrow the car for once, but my nerves were on high alert.

Why, why, why had I said yes to this place?

Because I didn't want to make a thing about it, that's why.

Still, going to this spot for my first date, with someone other than Marc, in more than three years probably wasn't the smartest move. It certainly wasn't helping my nerves. I twisted my left hand around my right wrist tightly.

Brandon is not Marc, I kept reciting to myself. He was my chance for something new, something incredible, and something I'd only get if I went in. *You've got this, you've got this, you've got this, you've got this*, I whispered, trying to psych myself up.

Did everyone feel this terrified going on dates? I needed to get inside. Brandon was probably there already. What if he saw me debating whether to enter? That wasn't how I wanted to start things. It was time. I could do this. I opened the door and went in. I did a quick scan and felt myself go clammy. I didn't see Brandon.

Was he standing me up?

I looked at my phone. No message. It was too early to get myself worked up, but I couldn't help it.

"Cam!" It was Brandon, leaning on the wall by the cash register. I let out a long breath. He was here.

"Hey."

"Hi," he said, straightening himself up. "They're clearing off a booth for us," Brandon continued as he walked over to me, his arms outstretched.

I guess that meant he wanted a hug. I could handle this. I stood up and gave him one. He squeezed tight, hanging on just a second longer than you would if it was just a friend thing. He smelled like peppermint and the outdoors. It wasn't what I was used to, but I was looking for a new go-to scent, and I wasn't going to rule this one out. The night was off to a promising start.

"Thanks for doing the article," he said as the waitress led us to the table. "Can't wait to see it. It's going to go right up on my wall."

I slid into the booth across from him. "I'm honored." I slapped my hands over my heart, but I did it so hard, I let out an *oof*. I laughed to try to cover it up. "So, yeah, it should be out in next month's edition, I think." What was wrong with me? I needed to stop panicking and just have fun. People went on first dates every day; this was no biggie.

"Nice," he said. "I'll look out for it."

Brandon was even cuter than I'd remembered. Dirty-blond hair, light brown eyes, and a sort of swagger about him. I hadn't thought much of him last year—he was just one of Marc's teammates that we didn't really hang around with—but he certainly had my attention now. "Should we get it over with?" he asked.

"Huh?" Get what over with?

"The picture."

Right. My excuse for meeting with him. "Yes," I said, and pulled out my phone. The truth was, the paper was probably going to use a shot from one of his games, but it wasn't a big deal. Extra photos were always good, and now I'd have a pic of my possible boyfriend on my phone. It was a bonus. "Smile."

He gave me a ginormous grin and I snapped the photo. Okay, he was *really* good-looking. How was I supposed to stay cool and breezy, like this was no big deal? "Looks great," I squeaked out.

"Now that we got that outta the way," Brandon said as the waiter came by and dropped off some water. "What should we get?"

"The milkshakes are amazing."

"I'm not so much a sweets guy."

"You're not?" I asked. Okay, it was all right. Just because dessert was my favorite meal of the day didn't mean I couldn't fall for someone who didn't like it. It just meant more for me. "What about mozzarella sticks, then?"

"That works," he said, studying the menu. "Want to share one of their appetizer samplers?"

"Sounds good."

We placed our order, and then he just looked me in the eyes, not saying anything at all. I felt a bit exposed, but I didn't turn away. I wanted him to know I was interested.

"Congratulations on your win," I said, breaking our eye contact when I felt myself getting jittery. The soccer team had won its game last night; it was their third win in a row.

"Thanks. Knew we were gonna. You should've been there. It was something else—I got like three assists and two goals," Brandon said. "You need to start coming to the games again. You're missing out."

He had to know about the breakup and how awkward it would be for me to be a spectator at my ex's games. I was sure the whole team had talked about what went down. "Yeah, well, don't really have a reason to go anymore."

"Maybe you will now," he said, and winked. It actually made me relax. It meant Terri had gotten me nervous for nothing. This was *so* a date. Brandon clearly knew it, and while I may have sucked at flirting, he certainly didn't.

I winked back. "Maybe. You never know."

"You must miss it," Brandon said. "I remember those giant posters of yours, the face paint and the screaming. Pretty sick."

I knew he meant it as a compliment, but it made me feel self-conscious. I had been to almost every game the past three years, cheering Marc on. It all seemed a little embarrassing now. "Guess I was hard to miss."

One side of his mouth raised in a little smirk. "That you were."

He noticed me? I mean, as something other than a highly overcaffeinated girl rooting for her boyfriend? The thought made me smile. It hadn't really crossed my mind that anyone on the team saw me as more than Marc's girlfriend, one of the guys, or a frenzied fan.

"I wanted you guys to win," I said.

"I heard. You were louder than the cheerleaders. It was cute."

The waiter dropped off our food, and I grabbed a fry.

"Hey," he said, "remember that screw shot I did last year in one of the first soccer games?" he asked.

My eyebrows furrowed, just momentarily, before I caught myself. I was surprised that he'd bring up some old play from a random game that nobody could possibly remember, but he took it as my not understanding the term. "You know what a bending free kick is? It's when you put a spin on the ball that makes it change direction."

"I know." I'd practically lived and breathed soccer during my Marc days. I just thought it was an odd thing to bring up now. Although I couldn't really complain; it wasn't like I was the queen of conversation at the moment.

"It totally changed the course of the game," he continued, and then rattled on about the play, either oblivious to the fact, or not caring, that my eyes were glazing over with boredom.

I picked up a mozzarella stick. "These are really good," I said in a sad attempt to change the subject. "I could eat them all the ti—" The word got stuck in my throat, and my skin got goose bumps, but not the good kind, not the ones from excitement over starting a brand-new romance. Those were the ones I wanted to have tonight. But no. The ones I was granted came from panic and shock. From noticing my ex and his date being escorted to a table in the same diner as me.

This had to be a joke. Only it wasn't.

Marc was at Scobell's with *Lissi*. First she tried to steal a spot on the volleyball team and now my boyfriend? My *ex*-boyfriend, I reminded myself. Ugh. I knew Marc was supposedly dating, but why did it have to be here and *now*?

My breathing picked up. Why was this happening?

"Cam?" Brandon asked.

I looked from my ex to him.

"You okay?" he asked.

No. No, I was not.

Do not look at your ex. Focus on the gorgeous guy in front of you. I repeated the directions in my mind, but it was easier said than done. The waitress sat Marc and Lissi a couple of booths away, on an exact diagonal from me. I wasn't sure if they saw me, but if they did, they didn't let on. They were holding hands across the table. Marc was nodding at everything Lissi said. She moved her hair behind her ear, and the way he lit up, it was like he was watching a private *Victoria's Secret* fashion show. It was puke-inducing. They were totally engrossed in each other. *Did Marc and I ever look like that?* We'd talked all the time, but I didn't remember us hanging on to every word the way they were doing.

"Cam?" Brandon said again.

Right, I had someone of my own. Better yet, someone I wanted Marc to see me with. Maybe this was a blessing in disguise. If I was freaking out over seeing Marc on a date, maybe he'd feel the same way.

"Sorry." I shook my head, trying to erase the memory of what I'd just seen. I needed to concentrate on Brandon. "Thought I saw someone. You should try the mozzarella sticks." It was all I could come up with to say. Clearly I wasn't going to get a gold medal for my verbal skills. I never should have dropped that persuasive-speaking class.

He took a bite of one, and cheese oozed out. He caught the excess mozzarella on his fork and twirled it around with a light laugh. "It almost got away there."

"It did," I said. I couldn't think of anything to follow it up with. What was wrong with me? I needed to do better. I took a giant mouthful of a mozzarella stick. It would keep me from having to talk, at least for a minute.

"Anyway," he said, jumping right back into his never-ending soccer story, "like I was saying, after that game, Coach started putting me in all the time."

I remembered that part very clearly. Marc had been so annoyed when Brandon started playing. He'd gone on about it nonstop. At the thought of Marc, my focus drifted back to his booth. I quickly snapped my attention back to Brandon. Or I tried to, anyway.

Why was I being such a fool?

Do not get distracted, Cam. So what if you can hear Marc laugh? So what if you can hear snippets of his conversation? So what if he's telling her about yesterday's soccer game, and how he butted the ball with his head and scored the winning point and now the team is one step closer to the championship game? There was no reason to care. If I wanted more boring soccer talk, Brandon was sitting right here.

"Right?" Brandon asked.

Oh crap.

I had no idea what he was talking about. I hadn't been paying any attention.

"Definitely," I said, figuring that was the right answer. Except, with my luck, I'd probably just said puppies were evil or that I wanted to go bungee jumping over a volcano or take a bite of a squid, beet, and anchovy pizza.

Brandon popped a fry in his mouth. "You know, when I was in middle school, everyone said I'd have to pay my dues in JV or take a back seat to the upperclassmen like everyone else, but I was like, 'Nah. They'll see.' And they did, ya know?"

He was still going on about that? "Sure," I said. "I—"

I was going to tell him how Grace got bumped to varsity at the start of her sophomore year, but I had barely started my story before he spoke over me.

"At tryouts, Coach pulled me aside. He was like, 'I need you on my team,' and I was like, 'I'm there.' He was hesitant to put me in at first, didn't want to piss off the other guys, but he came to his senses."

Do not check out Marc. Do not check out Marc.

"Mmm," I said when Brandon looked at me for acknowledgment that I was listening. Then he kept on going.

"I've been thinking about which college I should play at, making my dream list, you know?"

"Yeah."

Maybe it was the words *college* and *dream*, but my focus somehow made its way over to Marc again. But this time, our eyes met. I jerked my attention back to Brandon, who was still talking about himself. "I'm going to have my pick of schools. I'm going to blow up the soccer world," he said.

I didn't have to look to know Marc was watching us. I could feel his eyes on me. *Brandon* and me.

Ha! *How does it feel seeing your ex out with someone else?*

Marc being here wasn't messing up my evening. It was making it the best possible night ever. Payback. I could imagine what he was thinking: that this sucked. It was all well and good for him to be out with someone else, but me? No, I was sure he wanted me at home thinking about him. Everything was always about him, but not tonight. Tonight was about me and Brandon. It was time to make Marc understand how much it hurt when someone you loved went out with someone else.

"You are such a great soccer player, Brandon," I said, making sure to project my voice. "Best on the team." Take that, Marc.

Brandon's eyebrows furrowed, probably because my volume had tripled, but he took the compliment anyway and proceeded to tell me more about his best soccer plays.

It was like I'd accidentally left ESPN on and the commentator was droning on and on about games I had no interest in, but you wouldn't know that from looking at me. The glassy eyes were gone. Anyone watching would see a girl totally enraptured by her date's stories. I threw in some gasps and *no way*s, a few hearty laughs where I even tossed my head back for added effect, and kept my gaze locked on Brandon's. Marc was probably ready to explode.

I couldn't help it—I had to sneak another look to see.

I felt myself deflate. His focus was 100 percent on Lissi.

No, Marc was not going to win this. He was probably trying to make me jealous—well, the joke was on him. It wasn't going to work; I was going to be the one to come out ahead. I just needed to up my game.

"I am having such an *amazing* time," I said loud enough that I was sure to catch Marc's attention again. "Greatest. Date. Ever. Right?"

Brandon didn't answer. He was looking at me a little confused, but it didn't matter; Marc couldn't see his expression. Brandon's back was to him. Marc could only see *my* face, and as far as he knew, my date was fully enchanted.

"I'm so glad you agree," I answered for Brandon, but solely for Marc's benefit.

Then I took it a step further. I grabbed a fry, reached over, and tried to feed it to my date. In my head it was a sweet, romantic, *Lady and the Tramp* moment, but the reality fell short. Quite short.

Brandon was looking at me like I had lost it—his mouth had literally dropped open like he was trying to form words but couldn't—but that didn't stop me. Of course not. It was like I was on autopilot. I reached over and touched his arm. "So strong," I said. "I like it. I've never dated anyone as strong as you."

I was laying it on thick. Too thick, even for someone as ego-driven as Brandon, I realized just a smidge too late.

"What's gotten into you?" Brandon asked, pulling his arm away.

"Nothing." But when I said it, I must have glanced back at Marc, because Brandon followed my gaze.

"You've got to be kidding me," he said. "Is this some sort of game? Did you plan this? Did you know he was going to be here?"

I pulled my sweater slightly away from my chest. My whole body was overheating. I *really* hoped Marc wasn't watching this part. "No, you picked the place, remember? I didn't know. It's just a coincidence."

He shook his head. "This whole date you were just trying to make Marc jealous."

"I wasn't. Honest. I liked hearing your soccer stories." That part was a lie, but I was in a sinking ship here. "He just caught me off guard, but I'm having fun. Let's not ruin it. Are you a FIFA fan?"

"What?"

It was my last-ditch effort to get Brandon talking again, so I could try and save face in front of my ex. Marc was obsessed with the World Cup. Last year I'd spent the majority of my June and July watching the soccer championship. Chances were good that Brandon was a fan, too, and I needed him to stick around. I couldn't have Marc see my date implode; I wanted to make him jealous, not justified in his decision to dump me.

I picked up a mozzarella stick. "I was just thinking how much I love FIFA and figured you must, too."

Brandon nodded. "I do."

Maybe this would work—he was starting to talk again. I just needed to keep the conversation on soccer.

"I hate that it's only once every four years. They should totally make it two, right?" I asked. It'd been something Marc used to say all the time.

"Yeah, I'd be all for it—seriously, Cam?"

"What?" I asked.

"You're still looking over at him."

I hadn't even realized I was doing it again.

"I'm not," I said, dropping the rest of my mozzarella stick onto my plate and wiping my hands with a napkin. I'd unintentionally squeezed the life out of it, and oil and cheese dripped all over me. "I didn't mean to." I was worse than a moth to a flame. I'd just wanted to know if Marc was watching me. I hadn't meant to make the evening go up in smoke.

"You know"—Brandon took out some money and dropped it on the table—"some of the guys warned me not to go for Gerber's ex, but I . . ." He threw up his hands. "I'm just going to go."

"Please don't," I said. "I'm really sorry."

He stood up and shook his head, "That's . . . it's . . . I don't want . . ." He didn't even finish the sentence. "Good night."

I wanted to beg him to stay, to not do this to me. But I couldn't. I couldn't make another pathetic scene inside the diner. Especially not with Marc and Lissi there. I watched as Brandon walked away from me. This time there was no Avery to save me. This couldn't be happening again.

I refused to be the girl who got ditched at Scobell's twice. I needed a cover. I needed to do *something*. I grabbed my phone and pretended to talk into it. I waved to Brandon as he reached the door. "I'll be right there, just need to finish this call," I yelled out.

There was a good chance that Brandon thought I was insane, but I didn't care. I was not going to let Marc see me get ditched.

I pretended to chat for a minute; then I put my share of the bill on the table and got up.

I refused to look at Marc and Lissi. The irony was not lost on me that, had I done that earlier, I'd still be on a date at that very moment.

Instead I put on a smile, held my head high, and left the diner.

I was never coming back here again. I got dumped every time.

Except that tonight, I had no one to blame but myself.

Chapter 15

I parked the car in my driveway and texted Grace and Terri what had happened.

Moments later the phone rang. It was Terri. "Hang on," she said, "conferencing Grace in. This is way more than a text conversation."

"Cam?" Grace asked once she was added on. "Sounds like it was awful. Are you okay?"

"Yeah, the Marc-and-Lissi part of it sucked. But I can't say Brandon was a big loss."

"You mean he wasn't 'the one'?" Terri asked.

"Ha-ha." I leaned back against the headrest. Much to my disappointment, he really wasn't. Even if the whole Marc-walking-into-Scobell's thing hadn't happened and made me ruin the night, I still wouldn't have wanted Brandon. He had been all about soccer, and I'd already had more than enough of that to last me a lifetime. "He didn't even ask me any questions about myself." I guess I should have expected it. Our texts and emails had been pretty one-sided, too, but I'd credited that to the article I was working on. Of course he'd talked about himself then—I was doing a piece on him. I'd just thought that once that was out of the way, he'd be curious about me and ask questions about my interests. Or at least talk about something that didn't relate to soccer or himself.

"Anyway, enough about me. How are your nights?" I was done thinking about my evening. I wanted to hear what they were up to.

"Not as eventful as yours," Terri said.

"Definitely not," Grace agreed. "I'm just going over my Brown application."

"And I'm going to a movie with Steve in a little bit."

"The guy from the art store?" I asked.

"No, Steve Booker, from my study hall."

I needed a diagram to keep track of her social life. "I don't know how you do it."

"She's the master," Grace said.

That was the truth. "Teach me your ways, Obi-Wan."

"Huh?" Terri asked. "Is that your way of asking me for help? Because if it is, I'm ready for the challenge. Ooh," she purred. "I have an idea." Her tone made me nervous. I could almost picture her tapping her fingers together maniacally.

Apparently, I wasn't the only one. "This is going to be good. Whatever it is, count me in. I want to see this," Grace said.

I hadn't been serious when I'd asked for help, but I clearly needed it. I'd bombed on my own. I was just a little nervous about what Terri's tactics might be to help me find a guy. "What do you have in mind?"

Terri laughed. "Don't sound so scared. I'll take it easy on you. We'll start small. We'll go to the mall."

"The mall?" I asked.

"Yes, the mall," she answered. "The place is always crawling with cute guys, and not just ones from our school, but ones from the surrounding towns, too. I've met a bunch of people there."

"Smart," Grace said. "We should go tomorrow. Three o'clock?"

"Done," Terri agreed. "I'll pick you both up."

They spoke like I wasn't even part of the conversation. "Hey, don't I get a say?"

"No," Terri said. "After tonight, I think it's best that you leave everything to Grace and me."

She had a point.

"You guys are the best."

"We know," Terri said.

"Do you need some company?" Grace asked.

"No, you need to finish your application." I knew she wanted to get it done this weekend, and she was already taking time off tomorrow to come to the mall with me. Grace had been dreaming about going to Brown University almost as long as I'd been dreaming of living in New York. She was applying early decision, and while she still had plenty of time to get the application in, she was not one to wait around. "I have a few more pages left in my book, and I want to watch a movie."

"Let me guess," Terri said, "a rom-com?"

"You know it," I told her.

"Well," Grace said, "you can watch someone else get the guy tonight, but tomorrow we'll get you one of your own."

I smiled as we said our goodbyes. I really liked the sound of that!

Chapter 16

I laughed to myself as I headed up my walkway. My disaster of a date was going to make quite the lunchtime story. I couldn't wait to tell Avery, Nikki, and the rest of my cafeteria crew. It was strange—despite everything that had gone on tonight at Scobell's, I felt surprisingly good. I owed that to Grace and Terri. They always knew how to cheer me up. I wished I could do something for them in return.

Crap. That reminded me: I still needed to come up with a way to make Terri's family see that she belonged in art school. I just wasn't sure how to do it.

"Who is it?" my sister yelled as I fumbled with the lock.

I stepped inside. "It's me."

"Oh," Jemma said, relaxing back into the couch. "Mom and Dad went out. Why are you back so early? Must have been some date."

How did she even know I'd had one? I shook my head. She had to have been snooping again. I stole her bowl of popcorn and fell into the seat next to her.

She snatched it back.

"Why are *you* home?" I deflected. "Even Mom and Dad are doing something, and you're sitting here watching TV."

She folded her arms over her chest. "You mean like you are right now?"

"At least I had plans." I tried to grab the remote from her, but she clutched it like she was Gollum in *The Lord of the Rings*.

"I could have plans if I wanted to," she said. "I *like* being alone. Unlike some people in this room, I don't need to have twenty-four-hour supervision to be happy. Did you get Grace and Terri surgically removed from your hip? You know they'll just grow back in a second." She rolled her eyes at me. "Are you going to go see them now?"

"No, I'm going to sit here and bug you." I was about to add something snarky, but I saw her fight a smile. Then she passed the popcorn bowl to me.

Jemma wanted me there.

"So you really just wanted to stay home?" I asked.

She bit her cheek. "No."

I turned to face her. "What is it?"

"I'm not out because all my friends are at Dave's party," she said, her voice a whisper.

"Marc's brother Dave?" He was a year ahead of Jemma at school. She nodded.

"And you weren't invited?" I was angry. I couldn't believe he'd include all of Jemma's friends and leave her out. Worse, that her friends were okay with it. Grace and Terri never would have ditched me.

"No." She shook her head. "I was invited."

I felt a wave of guilt and love wash over me. She'd skipped the party because of me. "Jemma, you could have gone."

"I didn't want to be at the Gerbers' house. Not after what he did to you. I unfriended all of them," she said. I'd gotten rid of Marc on my social media accounts, too, but even I hadn't gotten rid of his brother.

I wasn't sure whether to laugh or cry at the look of determination on her face. It struck me, kind of all at once, how sweet it was that Jemma cared so much.

I moved closer to her and put my arm around her. "It's not Dave's fault, and I'm okay with you being friends with him. I don't want you missing out on anything else because of me, okay?"

Her mouth twisted, like she was trying to determine if I was telling the truth.

"Promise me," I said.

"Okay, fine."

"Good." Sitting there, I realized just how much I was going to miss her nosy, overdramatic, know-it-all self when I went to college next year.

I had a feeling she was going to miss me, too. I was definitely going to make an effort to spend more time with her, starting now. In a sneak attack, I grabbed the remote from her. Just because I was going to hang out didn't mean I was going to let her pick the show.

"Hey!" she yelled, tackling me in an attempt to get it back, sending the popcorn falling.

"You're cleaning that," I told her.

"No way," she objected, laughing as I reached the remote over my head. "Give it back. *The Real Housewives* is about to start."

I groaned. "No." I was not a reality-TV fan. "It's on all the time."

"Yeah, but they're about to go to an art show, and it's supposed to be 'explosive,'" she said, quoting the promos. "I can't miss that."

Jemma lunged again and got the remote from me, holding it up in victory. "I win!"

But I wasn't thinking about TV anymore. I'd figured out what to do for Terri. "Jemma, you are a genius." I took her head in my hands and kissed the top of it.

"Huh? I mean, yeah, but what are you talking about?"

"You gave me an idea to help Terri. I'm going to throw her an art show."

"Whatever," Jemma said, and turned up the volume on the TV.

I couldn't believe I hadn't thought of this sooner. Terri's parents needed to see all her work laid out at once. Sure, they saw her sketching, and a piece when she finished it, but maybe they needed more than that. Maybe they needed a gallery.

With Grace's and Luke's help, I could pull this off. I could already envision the gallery space in my mind. We'd make it epic. I shot Grace and Luke a text, then settled back down next to Jemma on the couch.

Chapter 17

Grace played with the straw in her Frappuccino and stared into nothingness as we sat in the mall's food court ready to map out our get-me-a-guy plan.

"Okay." I waved my hands in front of her face. "What is going on with you? You were barely there in the car, and now it's even worse."

"Sorry," she said, giving me a clearly fake smile. "It's nothing."

"It's something," Terri said.

Grace threw her head back. "It's stupid. Let's just focus on Cam and figure out where we go first. There's a group of guys by the Sbarro—you should be able to infiltrate that group, right? Get Cam an introduction?"

"No, no, no, no, no," I said. My love life could wait. Clearly, I wasn't the only one with drama in my life. Grace seemed to be swamped in it. "Okay," I prompted her, reaching for my charm bracelet before remembering it was no longer there, "talk. I want to know what's going on."

"It's just volleyball," she said. "Coach is letting *Lissi* play in the next game. He didn't even tell me. I only found out because Crystal texted me an hour ago. Lissi told her."

The name alone made my skin crawl. "How?" I asked. "I thought he was super strict about the rules."

"He found a loophole. Maddy Warmack said she'd be the team manager so that Lissi could take her spot and play."

I tried to remind myself that it wasn't Lissi I was angry at; she hadn't done anything other than go on a date with Marc. There'd probably be a lot of girls who'd be hanging out with my ex, and hating them all didn't seem like a good use of time. I wouldn't tell Grace, but the truth was I wasn't quite sure what was so horrible about Lissi wanting to play on the team. It must have sucked moving right before the start of senior year. It was bad enough she was going to have to make all new friends, but to go from being the star of her old team to not even having a team? That blew. I didn't blame her for wanting to play. I'd want to.

"Maddy never gets game time anyway," I offered up as a consolation. "It won't be that different for her."

"Exactly," Grace explained. "For *her*. It's the rest of us that are screwed. Lissi's not going to be a benchwarmer, so while she is technically taking Maddy's spot, in reality she's going to be pushing aside people who normally get to play. It'll mean less time on the court for players like me."

"That's crap," Terri said.

"Seriously." Grace squeezed her eyes shut. "I played up turning the team around and how the court was my home away from home in one of my college essays. That won't look so impressive if I barely even get to play my last year."

I squeezed her arm. "I'm sorry. It sucks, but I'm positive you have nothing to worry about. There's no way Coach is pulling you out of rotation. You're the star. The team would be nothing without you. I'll bet you whatever—all the ice cream you can eat, no snide remarks about whatever Halloween costume you choose for us to wear, homework for the rest of the year, whatever—that you'll have just as much game time."

Grace bit her lip. "Maybe, but that just means someone else gets screwed."

"It might not be as bad as you think," Terri said. "That person may not care about playing less. They may just like being on the team."

Grace looked skeptical.

"She's right," I told her. "That's why I liked it. Hell, if I'd known Coach was taking on a team manager, I'd have done it. Another extracurricular right there. Think I can fight Maddy for the job?"

Grace laughed. "*You* fight?"

"Yeah," Terri added, "my money is on Maddy. You'd be covering your head screaming, 'Not the face, not the face!'"

"Fair," I acknowledged, "although I'm a pretty good tackler." Jemma had learned her remote-control tackling skills from the best. On several occasions, I'd had to use my expertise to stop my sister or my friends from changing my movie choice. I didn't play around when it came to my rom-coms.

Grace laughed. "Yeah, I once thought I was going to have rug burn for life."

"Hey, that's what you get for trying to change *To All the Boys I've Loved Before* right at the best part."

"We saw that one like a hundred times," Terri protested. "Which means you've seen it a trillion."

"You can never get enough of a good thing."

Grace laughed. "I love you guys. Thank you."

I looked at her. "For what?"

She shrugged. "Taking my mind off things, making me feel better about the whole Lissi volleyball stuff. At least I don't feel like a total fraud in my college essay. I did not want to rewrite it. I'm done looking at it."

"Fraud, come on. Even if you decided to quit," I told her, "you wouldn't be a fraud. You're incred—wait! Did you finish?"

"Yeah, last night. The whole thing. Application is done and just needs to be submitted."

"No way!" I squealed. "You're a rock star—I can't believe you didn't say anything sooner. That's amazing! Congratulations."

"Thanks."

"Hey"—I blew a straw wrapper at Terri—"you're going to be her neighbor. I see you at RISD. I haven't forgotten my promise."

"And I haven't forgotten mine," she said, standing up. "Now let's go find you a guy."

Chapter 18

Terri, shopping bags in hands, threw her arms up. "What was wrong with that guy? He was hot! We've been walking around for an hour, and you haven't found anyone you wanted to talk to."

Grace took a bite of her pretzel. "I was right before. This is all too soon. You need some time to grieve Marc."

"No." I stopped and leaned against the wall. "That's not it. I'm done with him now. Seeing him last night brought me to my senses. I'm pretending he doesn't even exist. I'm over it. He doesn't mean anything to me."

I didn't need Grace's side-eye to tell me she didn't believe me. "Then what's the problem?" she asked.

I cringed. "I don't know how to do this."

Terri joined me against the wall. "Do what?"

I filled my cheeks with air and blew it out slowly. "Meet new guys, flirt, date. Last night was a mess, and you saw my texts with Brandon. I was with Marc forever, and before that we were lab partners, so we got to know each other; it was organic. This . . . trying to pick up somebody in the mall . . . feels fake."

"It's not," Terri tried to reassure me. "It's fun."

"It's terrifying." I'd thought coming here was a good idea, but it wasn't giving me the rush I'd imagined. If anything, it was just making me feel anxious. I looked around at the people near us. There was an old couple doing laps around the mall, a group of girls a little younger than us hanging out on a bench, a couple of cute guys headed to Jordan's, the electronics store. They definitely had potential, but I couldn't just go up to them and start talking. Who did that? I'd seem like a creeper. This was not like anything I'd ever seen in a rom-com. This felt scary. "What would I even say to someone?"

I should have thought of some lines ahead of time. What had made me think I could do this? I should have just had Terri set me up.

I clunked my head back against the wall.

"Just be yourself," Grace said.

Terri shook her head. "Nooooo, bad advice. She's panicking right now. She can be herself when she's on the date. Right now . . ." Terri turned her focus back to me. "I need you to be me. First, no slouching. Second, loosen up. Third, when you see someone you like, make eye contact, hold it for a few seconds, give a flirty smile, look away and then back to see if he noticed, then look away again."

"What?" I asked. She might as well have been speaking French.

"Don't be all Miss Innocent," she said. "You've read and watched how many rom-coms? And you're acting like this is a foreign concept to you?"

"Yeah," Grace said after finishing the last of her pretzel, "this should be easy. Just think of your favorite rom-com and emulate the lead."

"It doesn't work like that," I informed them. "Most of the stories you see me salivating over usually have a meet-cute or something; they definitely don't have the lead stalking a random guy in the mall."

It looked like Terri was fighting a massive eye roll. "Since we don't have a history paper for you and a stranger to team up on, or a sudden freak storm where you and Mr. Meet-Cute get to share an awning, how about we try what works in the real world? Seeing someone you like and starting a conversation. Last time I checked, that's not stalking."

I knew she was right, but it didn't make this easier.

"What if they don't want to talk to me?" I blurted out.

"Why wouldn't they?" Terri asked. She genuinely looked like she had no clue why I'd even think that, but my concern was warranted. Marc was the only guy who'd ever asked me out, and he'd dumped me for someone else. What if no one else would be interested?

"Hey," Grace said, reading my mind as usual, "they're going to be fighting over you. You're stunning, smart, funny, and an amazing friend who knows what she wants."

She could have been describing herself, but her Jedi mind trick worked. I finally budged from my spot on the wall. "Let's do this," I said.

Terri clapped her hands together. "Yes! Let's go to Jordan's first. It's like a haven for hot guys."

I followed them, the iced coffee I'd had earlier surging through my veins. *There's no reason to be nervous. There's no reason to be nervous.* I was still terrified, but I tried to hide it from them and from myself. How did Terri do this all the time?

"Them," she said, pointing out the guys I saw earlier.

"But there's two of them," I said, stating the obvious.

"Yeah, and three of us," Grace said. "We have them outnumbered. This will be easy."

"Just do what I said." Terri ran through her instructions again.

"Good posture, eye contact, smile, look away, look back, and onward." She demonstrated on me and made it look so easy.

"Fine."

The guys were over by the video games, reading the backs of a couple of them. The three of us walked by; I tried making eye contact with the shorter one, but he didn't even look my way. Neither one did. We kept going and regrouped near the cash registers.

I picked at a bowl full of USB drives shaped like Popsicles. "How are you supposed to give them googly eyes if they're not even looking in the right direction?"

Grace smirked. "Maybe it's good they weren't looking. Instead of googly eyes you might want to go for friendly or sexy, anything that doesn't scream Cookie Monster."

"I'm thinking Cookie Monster might have had better luck," Terri said. "He'd at least have asked the guys if they had any cookies. That's what you need to do."

"Ask them if they have cookies?"

Terri didn't need to speak; her look said it all—I didn't get it.

"If they're not looking," she explained, "you alter the plan and take the initiative. Say hi. Ask about the game they're holding. Anything!"

"You could have done it," I told her. "You could have gotten the conversation rolling."

"Teach a man to fish . . . ," Terri started.

I groaned. My father was always using that saying. *Give a man a fish, and you feed him for a day. Teach a man to fish, and you feed him for a lifetime.* It was what he'd spouted when he made me and my friends learn how to change a tire and check for oil, even though he barely let me use the car.

"I just need *one* fish!" I reminded her. "I'm not looking for a whole school."

She tossed me a heart-shaped stress ball from a container near her. "You'll thank me later. You need to learn how to do this. Talking to people is a skill." *Ugh.* Dropping that persuasive-speaking class was definitely a mistake.

Terri paused, stared at me, and then nodded. "It might be easier if you're alone. We'll wait in the next row. Just go walk up to them and start up a conversation."

I bugged my eyes out at her.

"Literally, all you have to do is say hi," she said.

"And what if they say hi *back*!?"

"Then you have a conversation." Terri spoke each word slowly, as if she were talking to a toddler.

"When did you get so shy?" Grace asked. "You gave those soccer boys hell for the past three years. They're like the hottest guys in school and you were always joking around with them, putting them in their place, and having fun."

"That was different." They were my friends; they were *Marc's* friends. I was one of the group, one of the *guys*. They welcomed me.

"It's really not any different," she said. "Just pretend the two over there are old friends, too, or, even better, people you don't care about. You can do this."

I squeezed the stress-ball heart and walked toward the guys. I could do this. It was for my future, and I was not going to be a wuss—not when it came to finding love.

I slowed down when I approached them.

"Hi."

The word came out of my mouth. It was me who had spoken it, yet this particular *hi* was a sound I'd never heard before; a frightening, high-pitched squeak that somehow got stuck in my throat, causing a sort of hiccup. I wasn't quite sure it was human. I had a feeling the guys didn't, either. They both turned and looked at me. I didn't stick around and wait for their reactions. I made a beeline for my friends, who were waiting for me in the next aisle.

"What are you doing here? Go back and talk to them," Terri whispered.

"Are you kidding me? Did you not hear what happened?"

Grace mimicked my squeal: "What do you mean?"

She and Terri laughed as I covered my face with my hands.

Terri pulled my arms down. "This is how you learn. Go back and start a conversation."

"I sounded like a mouse high on helium who also got stuck in a trap. I'm not going back there."

"You have to."

"Do it, do it, do it," Grace started softly chanting.

"You've got to be kidding," I said.

"I dare you," Terri challenged.

Grace let out a whistle. "Ooooohhhhhh."

They knew I couldn't resist a good dare. Still . . . this was asking for humiliation.

"You can't give up now," Grace said. "What would Bridget Jones do?"

I groaned. It was not fair to use Bridget on me. *Bridget Jones's Diary*, while an oldie, was one of my very favorites. I loved Bridget and the ridiculous situations she got herself in, but that didn't mean I wanted to re-create them.

Grace pointed her finger at me and donned a serious expression. "Do you want to be a disgrace to rom-com lovers everywhere? I don't think so. Now go back and finish what you started."

"Hear, hear," Terri said in agreement.

It shouldn't have worked. As far as motivational speeches went, Grace's was not the best, yet I found myself heading back to the row with the games—and the guys.

They hadn't moved; they were in the same spot I left them in.

"I love that one," I said, pointing to the game the shorter guy was holding, even though his body was totally blocking it from my view. I managed to speak like a human this time, although a slightly loud one.

He raised an eyebrow and waved the case at me. "*This?*"

It was one of those shoot-'em-up type of games. I'd tried similar ones a few times at Terri's house but always lost interest. I wasn't much of a gamer. Books, Netflix, Hulu, and the sort were my obsessions of choice.

"Yeah, it's great. I play it all the time," I lied.

The taller guy huffed, "It just came out the other day—there's no way you played it." Then he turned his back to me like I didn't exist. They both did.

"Whatever," the other one mumbled.

The tone, the move, and the dismissal made me fume. "Actually," I snapped, my mouth moving faster than my brain, "my mom is a 3-D animator, and when her company needs people to test new games, guess who gets to do it? And to think I was actually trying to help her find some fans to check out her next project. I should have just stuck with my friends."

Now it was my turn: I spun on my heels, giving them nothing but my back.

"Wait," one of them called after me.

I waved my hand back at them. "Too late."

I walked straight for the door, tossing the squished heart in the container by the cash register on my way, and left, my head held high. Terri and Grace got into formation behind me. We looked like the popular girls straight out of a teen movie.

"That was badass," Terri said when we were a safe distance from the store.

"Yeah," Grace agreed. "See, you can do this!"

They apparently needed to take some lying lessons from me. I had clearly upped my game. They, on the other hand, were not at all convincing. "Okaaayy," I said, complete with eye roll. "Not only did I not get the guy, I made a fool of myself."

"*What?*" Terri objected. "No you didn't. They were ready to chase you out of there. But who cares about them? They aren't the guys you want, anyway. This is about confidence and being able to talk to people. Yeah, you blundered. Since you're not a gamer, you may have wanted to go with 'is this game any good?' versus 'I play it all the time,' but it doesn't matter. You did something that scared you, and you didn't let them crap all over you. It was a win, a big one."

"I'm not so sure about that."

"Well, I am," she said.

"Come on." Grace put her arm around me. "It wasn't so bad, was it?"

"Yes," I told her. "It was tragic."

Terri put her hands on her hips. "Does that mean you're giving up?"

I shook my head, a smile forming on my lips.

"Oh no, I'm just getting started."

Chapter 19

"Next stop," I told Terri and Grace, "Orange Julius."

"Ahh," Grace said, "time for a pick-me-up? I could go for a DQ cone. Ooh, or a Blizzard. Or a Dilly Bar. Or all of them."

Just the idea of all that made me ill. "Your stomach never ceases to amaze me."

"Hey, you try practicing under Coach for almost three hours straight most days and see the appetite you build up."

She had a point. While I was moving a cursor around on a mouse pad, editing yearbook photos after school, she was doing drills and practice games. "You're right. You earn all the snacks you want. Hey," I said, getting another brainstorm. "I know we were joking earlier, but since Coach is being so welcoming all of a sudden, think he'll let me on the team so I can pad my résumé? I'll do anything. Assistant manager—I can help Maddy with whatever needs to be done. Towel picker-upper. Water pourer. Scorekeeper?"

Grace's face contorted. "Maybe." Her *maybe* didn't sound very convincing. "Coach doesn't like extra people around during practice," she explained. "He says it's a distraction, but you can try. It can't hurt."

I'd check in with him—there had to be something I could do for the team—but that was next week's problem. Right now was about meeting my future boyfriend.

"Come on," I said, ushering them toward the Orange Julius-Dairy Queen at the other end of the mall. "I need my drink."

"Since when do you like Orange Julius?" Terri asked.

"Since I realized they had a very cute guy working the counter."

Terri's eyes grew bigger. "What? How did I not see this boy? Don't tell me my radar is on the fritz."

"You were too busy ogling the display at the art store," I told her. The stores were right across from each other.

"And you didn't think to tell me? To call my attention to Mr. Orange Julius?"

I had thought of telling her after she came out of the art store, but I knew she'd have made me go talk to him. "I wasn't ready then."

"But you are now?" Grace asked.

I nodded. "Figure it can't go much worse than what happened at Jordan's."

A huge smirk crossed Terri's face. "I wouldn't count on that."

"Yeah." Grace elbowed me playfully. "Don't underestimate yourself."

"Ya know," I said, feigning mock outrage, "with friends like you—"

"You're going to wind up with amazing stories and a hot date," Terri finished for me. She jutted her chin toward the Orange Julius counter. "You weren't kidding. He's . . ." She didn't say anything else; she just fanned herself with her hand.

"Should we come with you in line?" Grace asked. "Or do you want to order for us, too, so you have extra one-on-one time?"

I debated my options. "How about you stand behind me, and if

I start talking like Minnie Mouse or do something else incredibly awkward, you guys jump in and save me?"

"Aye, aye, Captain," Terri said, and gave me a salute.

I saluted back and steadied myself before getting in line to meet Mr. OJ. He was really cute. Better than I remembered. He had this dorky-suave aura about him, if that was even a thing, and I was on board for it. He was lanky with straight dark brown hair that fell into his almost-aqua eyes, and the most charming lopsided smile I'd ever seen. I got in line and snuck another peek at him. He was saying something to his coworker that got them both laughing. I couldn't help but smile, too. A guy with a sense of humor—that would be a nice change. Marc had a lot of great qualities, but I never found myself having a giggling fit over something he said. Well, never something he said with the intention of being funny. This guy would be a trade-up. Added bonus, his eyes crinkled when he smiled. It meant it was real.

Standing in line was making me antsy. I needed the people in front of me to hurry up and order, I was more than ready to meet my potentially, possibly, hopefully, future boyfriend.

I finally made it to the front.

"Hi," I said to Mr. Orange Julius, trying my best to radiate rainbows and sunshine with my smile.

"I got this, Spence," the lady working the counter with him said. "You can get out of here."

Mr. Orange Julius, Spence, my chance at a perfect senior-year boyfriend, nodded and headed to the back of the store, completely out of view.

Noooooooooooooooo! I wanted to scream. *Noooooooooooooooo!*

He was leaving. Now what? Was I going to have to force my

friends or family to take me to the mall every day so I could stake out Orange Julius, hoping to catch him? This was bad.

"Did you want to order?" the cashier asked. She sounded annoyed, which meant she must have asked more than once.

"I guess. Umm, small Orange Julius."

"What flavor?"

"Huh?"

"What flavor Orange Julius? Orange? Tripleberry? Mango Pineapple?"

"Orange is fine," I said, stopping her before she named every item on the menu. I didn't care about the drink. I cared about the guy. The guy who was no longer anywhere to be seen.

I fished around in my purse for some cash while the woman prepared my order. This was a bust. The only thing I was getting out of it was a drink I didn't even really want.

Terri tapped me on the back.

I looked up. My drink was ready.

Terri tapped again.

"I see," I told her.

"No, you don't," she rasped. "To the left."

I turned. She was right: I *hadn't* seen. Walking away from the store—and me—was Spence.

I had to act fast if I wanted to catch him. I handed Terri my cash. "Take care of that for me, please. And I need that," I said, grabbing her art-store bag along with my drink.

"What are you doing?" Grace asked.

"Taking your advice." I looked back at her over my shoulder. "I'm Bridget Jones–ing it."

"What does that mean?" she asked.

She'd see soon enough. It meant I was going to turn my life into a real, honest-to-goodness romantic comedy. I wanted that happy ending, and I was going to do whatever it took to get it. If that included throwing myself into an outrageous situation, then so be it. If I couldn't have an organic meet-cute, I was going to have to fake it and hope things would go better than they had with Brandon.

I power walked until I was practically on top of Spence. It was now or never.

I paused.

Was I really doing this?

Yes, I was. There was no time for second-guessing.

I was all in.

I took that extra step forward, bumping into him, letting my purse, Terri's bag, and my drink fall.

"I'm so sorry," I said, a split second after it happened. "I wasn't watching where I was going. I didn't get you with the drink, did I?"

He shook his head.

But I already knew that—I'd been careful. I'd practically placed the drink on the floor so that it only slightly leaked out of the lid. I didn't want to make a mess, just a conversation starter.

Terri's things, however, had rolled away as planned. "Shoot," I said, and chased after a runaway little paint jar.

"Here you go," he said, collecting the other tiny jar, a paintbrush, a bag of sponges, and my purse. He was following my imaginary script to a T.

"Thank you," I said.

"No problem." He smiled that crooked grin, and I felt a little flutter in my stomach, one that made me go *Marc who?* "I think I have some napkins here." He pulled some out of his bag and handed me half the stack. We both leaned down to clean it up, and our heads butted together.

Ohmygodohmygodohmygod. Rom-coms could come true. This was perfect. It couldn't have gone better if I'd planned it myself—which, I guess, I sort of had.

We laughed and our eyes locked.

"I could get you another one if you want," he said.

"What?" I had been so focused on his eyes, I had no clue what he was talking about.

"The drink. I work there."

How do I move this forward? How do I turn this into a date? Do I just ask? Am I that bold? I had to decide quickly.

"That's right," I said, "I thought you looked familiar. I don't want to make you go back to work—you look like you're on your way out."

"It's not a big deal; it would only take a minute. My coworker probably already has one made."

Do it, Cam. Do it, Cam. Do it, Cam.

"I should be the one getting you a drink," I said, and tried Terri's trick of looking at him and then glancing away. "First I bumped into you; then you helped me with all my stuff. I kind of owe you one."

"I lived on Orange Julius all summer after I started working here, but then I hit my limit. I can't even stomach them anymore."

That wasn't on script. He was supposed to say, *I'd love that,* then get a drink with me, let his hand accidentally graze mine as he reached for it, until we walked side by side out of the mall into our happily-ever-after as sappy music played. I needed to get this back on track.

"We'll just have to go somewhere else, then," I said. Then I winked at him. *Who am I? Did I really just do that?* "Scoop Me Up has the best milkshakes on the planet." Somehow I was still talking, even if it was a half-truth. The ice cream shop had good shakes, but Scobell's were the best. They went extra heavy on the ice cream, but no way was I suggesting having another date there. Not after my last two experiences.

"I've been there, but never had a milkshake," Spence informed me, without giving me any clue what he was thinking—or if my attempts at flirting were working.

I forged on. "That's got to change, then," I said, half impressed with myself, half flabbergasted that I had this in me. "And hey, I do owe you one, right?"

He studied my face, his expression quizzical. Oh no. He thought I was weird, and maybe he was right. Maybe I should have left flirting to the Terris of the world. I wasn't cut out for this. Was it too late to make a run for it? If I was lucky, he'd beat me to the punch and just take off himself.

The seconds dragged on.

So much for my fairy tale. At least we'd each have a story to tell our friends. Although, in both versions, I was the one making a fool of myself.

"I'm Spencer," he said, extending his hand. "My friends call me Spence."

I shook it. *Yes!* He wasn't creeped out by me. "I'm Camryn. My friends call me Cam."

This was more like it. We even both had little nicknames. Totally adorable. Cam and Spence. Spence and Cam. Spam? That needed work, but we'd figure it out.

"I have to go meet my brother now, but a rain check on the milkshake?" he asked.

"Sure," I said.

Before I had time to debate if he was blowing me off, he offered another time. "I can do tomorrow if you're around."

Was I around? *Yes*, I was around!

"Works for me."

"Great, it's a date," he said.

A date!

We exchanged numbers and said goodbye.

As I watched him walk off, my friends, who had been eavesdropping nearby, rushed over.

We all started jumping.

"I have a date, I have a date, I have a date," I whisper-screamed.

Marc Gerber could eat his heart out. I had moved on to Spence . . . Spence . . . well, it didn't matter that I didn't know his last name. I'd learn it.

Chapter 20

As I got into the car to go meet Spence, I got a text from him: a GIF of a dancing milkshake. We'd been texting and sending ridiculous pics all last night. Most of them involving people bumping into things, dropping stuff, or falling over, but I also managed to learn more about him. For starters, his last name was Oswalt, he went to my school but we just hadn't crossed paths, he was a junior, and he had a giant sweet tooth just like me (as long as it didn't involve Orange Julius or Dairy Queen. He needed a break from them).

If the cute texts were any indication, our date was going to be amazing. I did a quick search and sent him back a GIF of the cutest-puppy-ever licking ice cream out of a glass.

Spence was already at the ice cream shop when I arrived, and his punctuality made me smile. Another thing he had over Marc.

I gave a little wave when I walked in. "Hi!"

Spence stepped forward, and I thought he was going in for a hug, so I moved in for one, too. Except that he wasn't. He was just standing there. Unfortunately, by the time I figured that out, I was three inches from him. I quickly backed up, but by this point he realized I had been trying to hug him, so he moved in for one.

It ended up being the most awkward half embrace, half pat on the back I'd ever encountered.

"Should we order?" I asked, hoping to quell some of the weirdness.

"Yeah," he said.

Neither of us spoke as we stood in line. I wanted to say something, but my mind was blank, so instead I pretended to study the list of flavors.

"What are you getting?" I asked, breaking the silence. Why wasn't this coming easily?

"I think I'm going to stick with a classic and go with chocolate. You?"

"I'm a mint chocolate chip girl."

Then it went back to silence until we ordered.

Once we got our shakes, we sat at a little table in the corner.

I took a huge sip out of mine. "This is sooo good. You have to try it."

His face momentarily contorted.

"What?" I asked. "Not a mint guy?"

"No, it's not that." Spence swirled his straw in his shake. "I have a thing about sharing drinks. I just really don't like it," he said in a rattling pace. "Back slurp kind of grosses me out. Which I know is weird because it's like, what if we kiss? I'm not weird about that." His eyes bugged out. "Not that I'm saying we're going to kiss. I'm just saying . . ." His whole faced turned as pink as the shop's strawberry ice cream. "I don't know what I'm saying." He slapped his forehead with his hand.

I laughed. "It's okay." In fact, it was kind of cute. "You know what this place needs?" I asked, hoping a change of subject would help relax him.

"What?"

"A mascot. A giant dancing milkshake." I opened my phone to the GIF he'd sent. "Couldn't you see someone dancing outside in a costume like this?"

"Yeah, but who'd want the job?"

"I'd do it," I said.

"No way."

"Yeah, getting people psyched about eating ice cream? I'd totally be the mascot." Then it hit me. I let out a gasp.

"What? What's wrong?"

Nothing was wrong. "I just had the most brilliant idea." I could barely contain myself—between the art show and this, I was on a roll. "I've been trying to build up my extracurriculars. I really want to do something with the volleyball team, and I just realized maybe I could be the team mascot! I'd be in a badger outfit instead of a giant milkshake, but same idea." Sam Raucher was the official mascot, Brooksy the Badger, but he was only at certain games for certain teams. Volleyball was never one of them.

"You're not serious, are you?" Spence asked.

"One hundred percent." The more I thought about it, the more excited I got. I couldn't wait to talk to Coach.

"That sounds torturous," he said. "Definitely not my thing."

"What's your thing, then?"

His whole face lit up. "You know e-sports?"

"Video games?"

"Yeah, but it's not just video games; it's taking it to a whole new level. Tournaments, competitions, audiences. My brother is an e-sports champ—he's won his last four competitions. I try to go watch when I can. He goes to college near here."

"Do you play?"

He nodded. "Yeah, I'm on the school's team. I hope to get as good as my brother or even better." Video games might not have been my thing, but Spence was passionate about them, and I liked that.

"Nice," I said. "Any other clubs?" I was always looking for ideas for new extracurriculars.

"Nah, e-sports take up most of my time. What about you?"

"I'm putting together the yearbook, wrote an article for the paper, and I know it doesn't sound like much, but I go to *a lot* of games. Volleyball, used to do soccer, and I go all out—signs, or shirts, or face painting."

"I've never been to a school game," Spence said.

I almost spit out the sip of milkshake I'd just taken. "Never?"

"I'm not a huge crowd person."

"The e-sports have a crowd."

"True, but except for my games and my brother's competitions, I mostly watch online."

"What about parties?" I asked.

"Not really a party person, either."

I slapped my hands on the table. "Come on, how can you not like parties? They're fun. You hang out with your friends, dance, not worry about school."

"They're crowded, noisy, you have to yell to hear anyone. I'd rather just stay home."

"I hear that," I said. I understood what he was saying; it was just the opposite of me.

That silence from before crept its way back in.

"Tell me about your favorite video game," I said before the quiet could overtake the rest of the date.

He started talking about *Warcraft III*, and I nodded as he spoke. Spence was nice. I liked him, but I wasn't sure he was the one for me.

After another half hour we got up to leave.

"This was a lot of fun," Spence said. For him it probably was; he had spoken about video games the whole rest of the time while I'd sat there and listened.

In his defense, I'd encouraged it.

Still . . .

I held back a sigh. It was looking like my hunt for Mr. Right wasn't over.

Chapter 21

Ms. Jackson stopped me as I headed out of last period on Wednesday. "I'm impressed with how hard you've been working."

"Thanks," I told her, adjusting my duffel bag on my shoulder. The yearbook was turning into a never-ending job. In addition to working on it in class, I'd stayed after school a bunch of days to get some more done on it. I still hadn't made a dent. I was going through the photos people sent in and putting together mock-up candid pages, as well as adding some extras to the team pages. But every day it seemed like we were getting a slew of new pictures. It was hard to make sure everyone from my class got represented. There were some people who seemed to be in every shot, and others who I barely saw in any pictures. At this rate, I was going to have to take some photos of my own or beg the no-shows to send them in. I still had time, though. I was saving a bunch of pages for senior-year stuff like the ski trip and prom. Hopefully, I'd get them in by then.

"I know it's a big project, but your photo retouching is wonderful," she said. "I'm still trying to get you some help. I think I may have a taker."

"Tell them if they have any questions, or need a push, to talk to me. I definitely wouldn't mind another set of eyes." It was weird being the sole decider (well, other than my teacher) of which pictures went into the yearbook. This was something people held on to forever. Sure, Terri and Grace would look it over, but I knew them, and they'd just say it looked great. I wanted someone who would point out if there were too many pictures of student X and not enough of student Y—or that I only noticed that my friend looked good in a shot, but that the person behind them was sporting a totally dorky expression.

"Will do," she said.

I glanced at the clock. The volleyball game was starting soon. "See you tomorrow," I told Ms. Jackson.

My phone buzzed. I cringed when I saw it was from Spence.

SPENCE

Let me know about Friday!

He'd asked me out again. I wasn't sure what to do. While our first date wasn't great, it wasn't totally bad, either. Maybe we just needed a do-over. I was tempted to try again, but there was a party Friday night that I really wanted to go to. I knew Spence wouldn't be game. We could just do another night, but then what? What if I wound up really liking him? I'd never go to a party with my boyfriend? I kind of hated the idea of that.

Now was not the time to think about it, though. I had a volleyball game to focus on. I shot Terri a quick text.

You and Luke don't have to save me a seat.

I'll be there. Promise. Prepare to be amazed 🐻 😛

I put away the phone. I'd been giving her hints that something was up since Monday, but I wanted my appearance at the game to be a surprise.

Avery, Nikki, and a few other cheerleaders were already outside the locker room by the time I got there.

"Sorry to keep you waiting. Ms. Jackson needed to talk, but I'm so glad you guys are here." After I had begged them during lunch the other day to help me out, they had agreed to cheer during the game. "Thank you so much for doing this. The volleyball team never gets the same attention as football or soccer, and they have a better record."

"No problem," Avery said. "Happy to help. Our other game is much later, and besides, I have a feeling this will be quite the show." She raised an eyebrow at me. "You ready?"

I patted the duffel bag. Was I ever!

We waited until the team was out on the court before we went into the locker room.

The cheerleaders changed into their uniforms as I took mine out of the bag.

"You're really doing this?" Nikki scrunched up her nose. "It's not too late to back out."

"Leave her alone," Avery chided her. "It's funny."

"And it's something to write on my application," I said, stepping into a giant, furry badger costume.

I had managed to convince Coach to let me be the school mascot, Brooksy the Badger, for the rest of the season's games. I'd run around, cheer, and get the crowd pumped every time the team won a set. It hadn't taken much persuasion to get the job. There weren't that many volleyball games left this year, and who didn't like a little school spirit? Besides, the school had a few badger costumes, so why not put one of the extras to good use, to not only help my college application but to support one of my best friends all at the same time?

I grabbed the costumed head. It looked more like a skunk than a badger. The thing was pretty hideous. The teeth and smile made it seem rabid, and overall it had the air of a haunted character at a deserted carnival. There was a good chance it was going to give me nightmares. "Rawr, rawrr, rawrr," I said as I put on the Brooksy head.

Nikki covered her ears. "What is that sound you're making?"

"It's the sound badgers make. I googled it."

"Never do that again!" she cried.

"Yeah." Avery cringed. "I may have to agree with her on that one. Although I do appreciate your authenticity."

Personally, I thought my impersonation was hilarious. "I'll think about it," I conceded as we neared the back entrance to the gymnasium.

"We going in?" Avery asked.

I peeked out to look at the scoreboard. "Once they win the first game. Let our appearance be a surprise."

It didn't take long. Brooksvale crushed Sandbrook. As the teams regrouped, I ushered in the troops.

"That's our cue, ladies!" I said.

We ran onto the court. The cheerleaders began one of their routines, and I jumped around trying to mimic them. They kicked; then I'd kick. They jumped; then I'd jump. I was three moves behind, and totally uncoordinated, but the crowd and the team were eating it up.

I'd thought dressing up as Brooksy would be amusing, but I hadn't expected the rush I got as I pranced around the court. It had been a long time since I'd performed in front of an audience, and I'd forgotten how exciting it could be. I was actually having fun. A lot of it. I decided to go all in! I turned my back to the crowd and shook my—well, Brooksy's—butt and did my best attempt at twerking.

I got a bunch of cheers and whistles, which only made me amp it up even more.

"That's enough, Brooksy!" Coach yelled. "Wrap it up. We have another set."

I gave a thumbs-up, the best I could in a costume, and ran to the sidelines. I was happy he didn't say my real name. Grace still had no clue it was me, and I wanted to see her face when she found out.

Sandbrook had nothing on Brooksvale. We were cleaning the floor with them. I jumped and screamed for every point. Especially when Grace was the one to score.

We were up 22–5. Crystal served. The other team returned the ball. Lissi bumped it, Grace hit it over, but the other team smacked it back. I thought we were about to lose the point, but Lissi threw herself onto the floor and got under the ball right before it touched the ground, putting it back in play. Grace spiked it over, and we scored! Grace and Lissi made incredible teammates, whether they—or I—wanted to admit it or not.

Two more points and we would win the next match. I ran over and gave Grace a high five. I even joined the huddle. After every point, won or lost, the team circled and everyone patted one another's back and said, "Go team," in unison.

This ritual was supposed to be team building, but I'd always thought it was silly and a waste of time. I finally understood. Even though they had no idea who I was, I was now one of the team, and I could feel the strong sense of camaraderie.

I put one arm around Grace, and the other around Crystal. "You got this," I told the team.

I had forgotten to disguise my voice, and Grace's mouth fell open as she turned to me in recognition.

I winked at her, but then remembered she wouldn't be able to tell through the costume, so I nodded. "Told you I'd find a way to get involved."

Then I started chanting: "Champions, champions, champions." My voice got louder with each repetition. Pretty soon I wasn't alone.

Grace was the first to join in, then Lissi, and then the rest of the group.

"Champions, champions, champions!" we all chanted.

At the same time, we all broke apart. The team took their places, and I went back to the sidelines, waiting for their win. It came easily, as did the one after that—which meant we won the whole set.

I took the court with the cheerleaders again, and this time I did a few laps around the gym, my arms in the air.

I ran into the stands all the way up to Terri, who was sitting in the back with Luke. She wasn't looking up; her head was buried in her sketchbook. I took her arm and swung it as I danced in front of her.

"What the—" she said, swatting me away.

I put on a fake booming voice. "What? You don't like Brooksy? Everyone likes Brooksy."

"Not me."

I started to laugh.

"Cam?" she asked.

"No way," Luke said.

"In the flesh—or rather the fake fur." I pulled off my Brooksy head. "Ever since Grace told us about Maddy becoming manager, I figured I could find a way to get involved, too. I already come to the games—might as well get some credit for it. So, voilà, here I am."

Terri shook her head. "I can't believe you didn't say anything."

"I would have thought my texts gave it away," I told her, putting one foot up on the bleacher and resting the Brooksy head on top of it.

"I wasn't paying attention. My head's been all over the place with my parents," she said.

I rested my furry paw on her shoulder. "I've got a plan."

"What are you talking about?" Luke asked.

"The art school stuff," I said.

He nodded. "Right."

"Wait," Terri cried, "Luke knows, too? You're in on it, aren't you?" she asked him, her mood picking up. "Tell me what you guys are planning."

I shook my head. "You, my friend, are going to have to wait and see. We're full of sur . . ." My voice trailed off.

"Cam?"

"Cam?"

Both Terri and Luke were calling me, but my attention went to the other corner of the gym. Marc was there. He never went to volleyball games. Not when I'd played, and not when I went to watch Grace play, never—but he was here now. I watched as he moved from his seat toward the court.

My Brooksy head tumbled to my feet.

Marc was here for Lissi.

He pulled her into a big bear hug, lifted her up, and spun her around.

I gasped as he lightly kissed her lips. This was way more than a one-date thing.

"Poor Cam," I overheard someone a few rows away say. "I can't believe Marc would do this. Throwing it in her face. You know, I heard he got with Lissi before school even started. Sometime in the summer."

I felt my chest tighten. *The summer?* Was that true?

"Are they a couple?" I asked.

Terri shook her head. "I don't know."

"Give me your phone." I punched up GroupIt. Terri had unfriended Marc, too, but his profile was public. I felt like the wind got knocked out of me when I called it up. He had updated his status. It said "in a relationship with Lissi Crandall."

How long had this been going on?

Memories came tumbling back to me. Todd saying Marc had traded up. All the lunch conversations from the first week of school. All the soccer guys talking about how hot Lissi was, how cool, how perfect. Had Marc been with her that whole time? Had the guys all known? Was I the butt of their jokes? They'd probably had a good laugh while Lissi waited in the wings.

Grace had been right: The girl totally sucked. So did Marc. I hated them both.

I could feel my cheeks flaming. It was bad enough when I thought Marc had ended things because he wanted to have a wild last year of high school, but because he liked someone more than me? That hurt. A lot. Marc didn't want to be free senior year; he wanted to be free of *me*. He liked having a girlfriend as long as she was someone else.

I felt frozen in place. "Hey," Terri whispered, linking her arm with mine. "Let's go."

Luke picked up Brooksy's head, and somehow my brain sent the message to my feet to walk.

But a headless badger didn't exactly go unnoticed making her way down the bleachers, especially when her ex-boyfriend was hanging out with his new love mere feet away.

All eyes turned to me. Including Marc's and Lissi's.

I stared back, my gaze icy.

Screw them.

I wasn't going to give them the satisfaction of seeing me upset. I brushed past them like they didn't exist and went straight out the door. I walked past the locker rooms and turned at the end of the hall, until I knew no one from the game would accidentally spot me. Luke, Terri, and Grace were on my tail.

"Marc's stupid," Terri said. "Lissi has nothing on you."

"She's gross," Luke chimed in. He was lying, Lissi wasn't gross; she was—as the soccer guys said—"the type of girl we dream about." I, apparently, was the type of girl who didn't even know when she was being played.

"Cam, say something," Grace said.

What was there to say? I tried to quiet the memories in my head.

"I'm fine." *I don't care*, I reminded myself. "She can have Marc. I don't want him anyway."

I was moving on.

I reached through my costume to my jeans and pulled out my phone.

I had Spence. He was so much better than Marc. So what if our date hadn't been perfect? Everyone had first-date jitters. I'd seen him make his coworker double over laughing; he'd show me that part of himself, too. He just needed to get comfortable. He was a good guy, and I deserved a good guy.

I started typing.

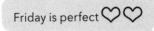

I didn't need to think twice.

I hit send.

I was done with the past; it was time to go after my future.

Chapter 22

> **TERRI**
> Get your butt over here.

It was the thirtieth text I'd received from Terri in the past five minutes.

> You know I can't.

> **TERRI**
> You mean won't.

Not this again.

A second later, she was FaceTiming me. "Look around me," she said. "This is where you should be. It's where you want to be." Terri was at the school for the dance. It was pretty packed, more than what I'd expected for an event in the gym.

She'd been giving me a hard time about skipping it. It'd been just over two weeks since I'd found out about Marc and Lissi being an official couple, and Spence and I had been hanging out a lot. We were about to have our fifth date. Terri had a lot of opinions when it came to that. She thought I was going out with Spence solely because Marc was in a relationship and I needed to prove something, but that wasn't true. Spence was a good guy, and I wanted to give him a fair shot.

"Cam," she said.

"You know I can't come. Spence hates crowds."

"Yeah, but you don't."

I covered one hand over my ear. "I can barely hear you with all that music." It was a lie; I just didn't want to have this conversation for the umpteenth time. Terri apparently didn't feel the same way. She moved into the hall.

"He's making you boring," she said.

"No he's not." I grabbed my lipstick and keys and threw them in my purse. "You know I want to be there with you. Don't make me feel guiltier than I already do. Come on, I have to finish getting ready; he's going to be here in a few minutes."

"Yeah, to bring you back to his place to play video games. Do I need to remind you that you hate video games? Whenever I try to get you to play, you make a face." She pointed at the screen. "That one. The one you're giving me right now."

"I'm making a face because you hate Spence."

"Overdramatic much?" Terri asked. "I don't hate him. I just wish you were here and blame him for keeping you away," she whined.

"Now who's being overdramatic?" I countered. "It's not like I don't see you practically every day. The dance isn't everything."

"Yeah, well, you're one of my best friends. I want you around, and it's not just me. Everyone is asking for you."

I could still hear the music playing in the background, and I felt a pang of regret for not canceling on Spence. "I think you'll manage."

"You don't know what you're missing," she said in a tone meant to entice me. "Luke asked Paisley Solloway to dance. It was the most awkward thing ever, but she said yes. Now they are attempting to move to the beat, and it's a geektastic sight to behold."

I did kind of want to see that, but I'd just have to hear more about it later. "Take pictures. Or a video," I told her.

"Nope," she said. "It's the live show or nothing. Come on," she pleaded again, "can't you stop by for just a little?"

"Terri . . ."

"Fine," she said, "I'll let everyone know you've turned into a grandma who hates to go out." She looked like she was walking.

"Oh, stop. It's one night."

"A night you were looking forward to! And it's been more than that. It's—"

A horn beeped. I was relieved. The last thing I needed to hear was her tearing into me for missing a couple of parties and pizza outings.

"Terri, I got to go. Spence's here. Have fun tonight. Tell everyone I miss them."

She fanned the camera around so I could see her surroundings. She was back in the gym. "Tell them yourself."

I waved.

Luke and Paisley waved back. They did look cute together. Grace said, "Stop by." And then Avery and a bunch of people I couldn't make out all cheered, "Yeah, come."

I threw them all a kiss. I loved that they wanted me there, even though I knew I had to turn down the invitation.

"Next time," I promised them. "Gotta run. Have fun."

I hung up and raced out to Spence's car. I leaned over and gave him a kiss on the cheek. It was these little moments that I wanted back in my life. The simple things: texts with hearts in them, an arm around me while we watched TV, someone to say *I love you* to. "Sorry for the wait. I was on the phone with Terri. She's at the dance. It looks fun. Maybe we can stop by for a few?"

Spencer shook his head. "Oh God, no."

I gave him puppy-dog eyes. "Just for a couple of minutes to say hi? It's on the way."

"What's the point of going for a couple of minutes?"

I tucked my hair behind my ear. "To be social, to see people."

"We saw them this afternoon at school." He groaned. "You're not going to make me go, are you?" Now he was the one giving big doe eyes. "I told you I hate those things. Please tell me we don't have to go."

I didn't answer, so he kept talking.

"I thought we said we were going to stay in and have you try some of the eGames. I thought that's what we wanted, right?" He gave me that crooked smile of his.

"Yeah, you're right. It is."

We passed the school as we drove to Spence's. My gaze lingered on the building. I shook my head. I didn't need some school party; what I was doing was better. I was spending time with a guy who liked me, a guy who could become my *boyfriend*.

We were going to have a good time. *A great time*, I reminded myself as the school pulled out of view.

This was what I wanted.

Chapter 23

"You're getting better," Spence said after finishing our umpteenth video game.

I dropped my controller on the coffee table. "Practice makes perfect, I guess."

It was fun. Sort of. I mean, I didn't hate it, but I couldn't stop thinking about everyone at the dance.

"How about we put on *Ant-Man and the Wasp*?" Spence asked.

"Again?"

He laughed. "The one we watched the other day was *Ant-Man*; this one's different. You'll love it."

I wasn't so sure about that. I didn't want to burst Spence's bubble—he seemed so excited to introduce me to this movie—but I'd had my fill of Marvel. Don't get me wrong, I liked superhero movies as much as the next person, but we'd only been out a handful of times, and we'd already watched four. I finally understood how Grace and Terri felt when I'd make them sit through rom-com after rom-com.

My phone buzzed, and I snuck a peek at the text.

"Everything okay?" Spence asked.

Shoot. I hadn't meant for him to see me reading my message. "Yep, my friends are going to go grab some food."

"Nice."

He was right, it was nice—and I wanted to be a part of it. Even if I hadn't been back to Scobell's since the Brandon fiasco. "You know, I could eat something."

Spence jumped up and bowed. "At your service. I have ice cream, chips, a spicy pasta chicken thing my dad made that tastes a lot better than I'm describing it, I can make us some mac and cheese . . . any of that sound good?"

I loved and hated that he was being so sweet. While what he was offering was super adorable, he was totally missing what I was trying to say. I needed to spell it out. "I was thinking we could join everyone at Scobell's."

"Oh." Spence sat back down.

"You don't want to . . . ?" It was more a statement than a question.

He rubbed the back of his neck. "Not really."

How horrible of a person would I be if I went anyway? We'd been on our date for almost two hours. That was a decent amount of time. It wouldn't be like I was ditching him. After all, I'd already given up the dance for him. How much was I expected to miss out on for a guy I didn't even know I'd have another date with?

Spence shrugged. "If you want to go, you should go."

I sat up straighter. "Really?"

"Yeah." He looked down and his hair fell over his eyes. "I don't want to *make* my girlfriend hang out with me."

My mouth fell open. Had I heard that right? "Your what?"

Spence's face turned red. "I . . . um . . . only if that's what you want . . . I just thought . . . we've been hanging out so much these past couple—"

"Yes!" I interrupted. "It's what I want."

Spence gave me one of his giant crooked grins, and I melted.

I had a boyfriend again. Everything felt right.

I moved closer to Spence and snuggled up to him. "Let's watch *Ant-Man and the Wasp*. I'm not going anywhere."

Chapter 24

"I talked to Terri. She checked with her parents—the date for the art show works for them," I told Luke and Grace before the volleyball game on Tuesday. "Looks like we're good to go. Luke, are you sure your family is okay with this?"

"Yeah, not a problem," he said, leaning back on the wall of the gymnasium.

Luke had been able to secure a private room at his aunt and uncle's restaurant for Terri's art show. He said they'd even comp everything. It was a pretty huge deal. The restaurant was pricey. Normally they required a huge deposit, and a minimum order that was way above our budget, just to reserve the space.

"Thank you so much."

"And you'll be okay getting the art?" I asked Grace.

"Yep," she said. Grace lived a few houses away from Terri, and her job was to collect the pieces for the show while Terri was out. Mine was putting together the presentation cards and booklet.

"I should go sit," Luke said, "before she gets here and sees us talking. I can't take a whole game of her trying to pry information out of me again. If she sees us all together conspiring, I'm doomed."

"Whatever you do, don't tell her," I said.

"I won't."

I looked out at the stands. No sign of Terri yet; we'd all made a point to get there early.

"Hey." I pointed to the last bleacher. "Is that Derrick?"

"I guess so," Grace said, looking away and biting her lip.

"Are you two back together?"

Grace shook her head.

"What's going on?" I asked. She was definitely not telling me something.

"I don't know why he's here."

"It has to be for someone on the team," Luke said. "You don't just come to these things for fun. No offense, Grace."

"None taken."

I felt my stomach thud. I really hoped Derrick wasn't dating one of Grace's teammates. She didn't talk about him much anymore, even when I pried, but on the rare occasion that she did, you could tell she still liked him.

"Should we go talk to him?" I asked. Maybe he was here for Grace, to win her back. Wooing her through her volleyball games—that would be so sweet. I could see the rom-com version of it in my head.

"No, I'm fine. Besides, we have to get ready for the game."

"Okay."

We went and got changed, me into my badger costume, Grace into her volleyball uniform. The game went smoothly. Not only did we win, but there was no sign of Marc. Fortunately, he'd had soccer today, and as for Lissi, I avoided her at all costs. To my relief, the volleyball season was almost over. It wasn't that I hated being Brooksy. I actually liked running around and performing in front of a crowd. And I *loved* that it was beefing up my résumé and college application.

It was even a possible essay topic. I just didn't want to deal with having Lissi around anymore. I was ready to be done with her.

After the game, Grace gave the rest of the team a pep talk in the locker room as I sat on a nearby bench, stuffing my Brooksy costume back into its duffel bag. "Guys, that was incredible," she said. "We have to keep it up. We're so close. We win the next one, we're in the championship. First place, here we come!"

They started whooping it up.

"And thanks to our captain," Lissi said.

I rolled my eyes. *And thanks to our captain*, I mimicked silently. Now she was trying to kiss up to Grace? Good luck with that. Grace wasn't going to fall for it.

The team cheered again.

When it quieted, Lissi kept on speaking. "I know I pushed my way onto the team, but thank you guys for having me. It's made moving here a lot easier. I love you guys almost as much as my old team." Then she laughed. "Maybe even more if we get the championship."

They were all laughing with her. "We're closer to getting there because of you," someone said. Then they all started feeding into her ego. My eye rolls quadrupled, not that anyone noticed.

Even *Grace* started participating. "Glad to have you here," she said. "Sorry if I gave you a hard time in the beginning."

I froze. *Seriously?!* What was she doing? Making peace with the enemy?

I kicked myself. I should have come to the practices, not just the games. I'd given Lissi an opening to move in on my best friend.

"No, I get it," Lissi said. "I wouldn't have liked it if the situation was reversed, but I am glad to be a part of the team. Hey," she added, "let's go celebrate our win. Scobell's, maybe?"

Okay, that was it. I flung the duffel over my shoulder and went to my locker. I wasn't sticking around to watch this. It was too much. First Lissi got my boyfriend; now she wanted Grace? What was next? Was she going to try to mentor my sister? Hang out with my parents?

I shoved the bag into my locker. It barely fit, but pushing it with all my strength was a release. I just pretended it was Lissi.

I felt someone behind me before I heard the voice—Lissi's voice.

"Cam, can I talk to you for a second?"

I did not want to turn around. What could she possibly want? To tell me how much fun she was having with Marc? To rub my nose in all the things she had that I didn't?

"What?" I finally asked, hoping there wouldn't be a response, that I somehow took long enough to answer that she gave up and left.

No such luck. I heard her breathing.

"So, I've been talking to Ms. Jackson, she's looking for people to help on the yearbook, and I told her I'd do it," she said at warp speed. "She told me to talk to you. I didn't know it was your thing when I first volunteered; if you want me to back out, I can."

Lissi was the student Ms. Jackson had been talking about.

Of course it had to be my archnemesis—well, the one in my head, anyway.

How was I supposed to answer her? What was I supposed to say?

I pressed my locker door shut, letting my hand rest there while I thought. I was coming up empty.

I turned around. Lissi wasn't the only one waiting to hear my answer.

Grace and the rest of the team were watching us like we were some gripping drama on the CW.

If I told her no, I'd look petty and jealous. If I told her yes, then I'd have to work with her. It was a lose-lose situation.

I looked over at Grace. She gave me a little nod. I knew what she was thinking. She wanted me to say yes. Of course she did, she'd apparently already befriended Lissi, but I wasn't feeling quite as charitable.

I turned my focus back to Lissi. "You know it's not that exciting, right? It's mostly just going through pictures and playing with Photoshop."

She nodded. "I know. I did yearbook back home. I mean, at my old school."

I took a deep breath. "And you'd have to work with *me*."

A few people around us snickered. Out of the corner of my eye, I saw Grace elbow someone.

"If you want me to tell Ms. Jackson I can't do it, I will." She didn't say it cruelly. Her voice actually sounded kind, if that was possible.

Unlike Lissi, who looked all graceful and calm, I had become a fidgety mess. I grabbed on to my locker to steady myself. "Do you want to work on it?" I asked.

"Yeah, I do," she said.

For the life of me, I couldn't figure out why. Who would want to take on a thankless project where they would have to deal with someone who hated them?

I wanted to say no, that I didn't think it would work, that it would be too hard, yet that's not what popped out of my mouth.

"Fine," I said, "you can work on the yearbook with me."

Chapter 25

"You did the right thing," Grace said, once we got to Terri's car and away from the rest of the team. I had taken off right after the Lissi debacle, followed by Grace. I hadn't spoken a word since. "Cam?" she asked, noticing my silence.

I whipped around so that we were face-to-face. "Don't you have somewhere to be? Like Scobell's with your new buddy?" I asked her, letting the sarcasm drip from my voice.

Luke came over just then. "Terri will be here in a few; she's just grabbing something from her locker." He looked from me to Grace. "Did I walk in on something?"

"Oh, you know," I said, "Grace and my ex's new girlfriend are like this now." I crossed two fingers together. I don't know what I was more pissed about—that I was stuck working with Lissi or that my best friend was acting all chummy with her.

"Lissi?" Luke asked. "I thought we hated her."

"We do," I said. "At least some of us do."

Grace threw her arms up. "Cam, come on. You're not being fair."

"*I'm* not being fair?" I whisper-screamed so that no one passing by would hear us. "I got dumped. She took my boyfriend *while* we were still together. And now you're advocating for her?"

"I'm not her advocate. I just think you're taking it out on the wrong person. She wasn't the one who did this to you. Marc did."

Luke backed up. He didn't want any part of this conversation. He was smart.

I could barely even look at Grace. "I can't believe you're taking her side. You saw me after the breakup."

"It's not sides," she protested.

"You couldn't stand her at the start of the year," I reminded her.

"Yeah," she said, "I know." Her voice was calm and even. "I was jealous and worried about my spot on the team. I took it out on her. It was wrong, and you're doing the same thing. *She* didn't do this to you. It's not about her."

I sucked in some air. Deep down, I knew she was right. I knew this was about Marc, but it was easier to blame Lissi for everything. She wasn't the one I'd loved. Who wanted to admit that the guy you would have done anything for was the one who'd made your insides feel like they'd been blended by a food processor? Maybe it wasn't fair, but why did it have to be? Lissi got the guy; I got the broken heart. She was still getting the better deal.

"Say something," Grace said.

"Like what?"

"Like that you know I'm right."

I looked up to the sky. "Fine, you're right. It doesn't mean I have to like her."

"No," she said, "but picture yourself in her shoes. It's hard being new, especially for senior year."

I bit my tongue. That's what I'd thought when Grace was spiraling out about Lissi, back when I didn't know about her and Marc being a couple. But I'd never made her feel bad about it. "Fine, go be her friend. Whatever. I'm not stopping you."

"Cam, it's not like that. It's just—I'm the captain; she's on the team. You're on the team, too. I want everyone to get along."

"Then she shouldn't have started dating my ex-boyfriend." I held up my hands. "I know, I know." It wasn't like I couldn't see that I was being unreasonable. It wasn't like I really expected Grace to shun anyone; it was just hard seeing her with Lissi. I'd get past it.

"If it makes you feel better, I'm skipping Scobell's," she said. "We can do something instead."

I shook my head. It didn't make me feel better—it made me feel like a spoiled brat. "No, you should go. You're the head of the team; you need to be there."

"Will you come?"

"Don't worry about me. I'm good. You can ignore that temper tantrum; I was just being a baby. You're the captain. I want you to enjoy it." I made a face. "Even if that means hanging out with Lissi. But," I warned her, "you can't like her more than me. Deal?"

"Deal." She came over and wrapped her arms around me in a giant hug. "That could never happen. Besides, I'm the one who should be worrying about Lissi replacing me. Volleyball's almost over. You're the one who is going to be spending all that time with her."

"Wait, what?" Luke asked.

I'd almost forgotten he was here, witnessing my little hissy fit. I filled him in on the yearbook stuff.

"That's . . . that's . . . going to be something," Luke said. Understatement.

"Need a ride to the diner?" Crystal yelled out from her car.

"Yeah," Grace called back. She turned to me again. "Please come. You missed Scobell's the other day; don't skip today, too."

"You'll make sure Lissi and I are at opposite ends of the table?" I asked.

"Promise," she said.

"Fine, I'll go."

Lissi had already taken so much. I wasn't giving her this, too.

Chapter 26

A lot of my free time had been devoted to Spence, but Thursday night was all about my friends. We were having a girls' night at Avery's house.

Her cousin had a tiny part in a movie that had just dropped on Netflix, and she'd invited a bunch of us over to watch it. Nikki, Meg, Naamua, Grace, and Terri were all going to be there.

"Cam!" A chorus of calls greeted me when I walked into Avery's basement.

"Sorry I'm late. Something happened with my mom." It was a little white lie. Spence had wanted help with his history report, and I was running behind schedule. I'd wanted to be at the party on time, but I couldn't run out on Spence when he was freaking out about finishing. So I stayed until he was in a good spot. I would've done the same for anyone; it wasn't like I was choosing Spence over them. It was just work versus fun, but I wasn't sure they would see it like that, and I wasn't looking for a lecture.

"Don't worry," Avery said, "we haven't even started the movie yet. We got a little distracted."

"Sit, sit." Terri patted the spot next to her. Everyone was in a circle on the floor, gathered around Avery's laptop, laughing.

"What are we looking at?" I asked.

"Pictures from the dance and the diner," Avery said.

Nikki pointed to one and squealed. "I can't believe you got that."

"I can't believe you did it," Avery countered.

They were all doubled over in laughter.

I glanced around. They were all in on it but me. "What?" I asked. "What happened?"

"We may have played a little game of truth-or-dare," Grace said, grabbing a handful of popcorn from a bowl in front of her.

"More like just dare," Terri corrected her, and they all started laughing again.

"Yeah?" I picked up a kernel that had fallen on the carpet and rolled it between my fingers. Inside jokes were great and all, unless you were on the outside.

Once the laughter subsided, Nikki said, "At the dance during one of the slow songs, when things were quiet, I had to sing my heart out."

"And we did the backup," Avery said, pointing to herself and the other cheerleaders. "But you know that's not what we're talking about. We wound up continuing the game when we went to Scobell's, and she . . . we . . ."

It was hard to even make out what she was saying through her giggling fit, but it wasn't just Avery; they were all having a laughter attack.

"You went to Scobell's? What's so funny about that?" I put on a forced smile. I felt like a spectator at a game I knew nothing about, with no one to explain it to me. I knew it was my fault—they'd invited me to hang out, and I was the one who'd chosen not to go because I'd made plans with Spence—but I felt like an outcast in a group that I'd formed. Terri and Grace never would have been this close to Avery if I hadn't merged us into one unit.

Terri flung her head back. "It started with this one." She pointed to Grace. "She made me go to a table that had ordered pancakes and ask if I could have a bite since I was thinking about getting them myself."

"You didn't," I said.

Grace fell over, her head landing on my shoulder. "Oh, she did, and then she got payback."

"I made her go back over to them," Terri explained, "and ask if she could have a bite, too."

"But this, this . . ." Avery couldn't even speak she was laughing so much. "This is where it gets good. The guys sent over a plate of pancakes, and . . ."

"What?" Getting this story out of them was excruciating.

"Okay, you know that old rom-com you made us watch?" Terri asked.

No. There were millions.

"The one where they're friends," she continued. "Harry and somebody."

"*When Harry Met Sally*?" I asked.

She tapped her nose. "Ding, ding. Well, you know the scene in the restaurant?" I did. The lead, Meg Ryan, a romantic-comedy staple, fakes an orgasm from eating a sandwich in the middle of the restaurant.

Nikki put her hands over her face. "I did it."

My jealousy over missing out was replaced by shock. "You didn't!"

"I did."

"They asked us to tone it down or leave," Terri said, and they all started cracking up again.

"You guys almost got kicked out of Scobell's?" No one got kicked out of Scobell's, not that I'd ever seen.

"She was *really* loud," Avery said.

Nikki shrugged. "Well, if you're going to put on a show, you've got to commit."

"I can't believe I missed it."

"Some of it's recorded for posterity," Avery said.

Except that wasn't the same; we all knew it.

Eventually we moved on to talking about other things, but I couldn't get their laughter out of my head. They hadn't even told me about this stuff until now. Just because I'd been busy didn't mean I didn't want details.

"Hey." Grace tossed a piece of popcorn at me. "You okay?"

"Of course."

But she knew what I was thinking. She always did.

"There's going to be more dances and nights out," she assured me, "and you're going to be a part of all of them. Oooh!" Grace clapped her hands together. "I have to Venmo Crystal money. Did you do it yet?"

"Your volleyball thing?" Terri asked.

Grace nodded.

The season was nearing its end, and the whole team was going up to Crystal's lake house for the weekend as one last bonding experience before the finals. Everyone was pitching in for food, gas, and even matching T-shirts. They were leaving after practice tomorrow.

Grace was still waiting for me to answer.

She was not going to like what I had to say. "I was going to tell you: I'm not going to go. I let Crystal know."

Her whole face fell, and everyone was watching us now. "Why?" she asked.

"It's a lot of money, and I'm not really on the team."

"What are you talking about? Of course you are! You're at every game, cheering us on, joining our huddles—everyone loves you."

"I'm not at every practice," I reminded her. "It would be weird for me to go."

Grace shook her head. "I'm the captain, and I'm telling you, it's not. Text Crystal right now. You can still go."

"Yeah, but Lissi's going to be there . . ."

"So what?" she said, pleading with me. "You hung out with her at the diner after the game."

She wasn't helping her case. Grace had stayed true to her word about keeping Lissi away from me at Scobell's. We were at opposite ends of the table, but it almost didn't matter. The whole meal felt like the Lissi show. She was telling stories, making the whole table—minus me—laugh, and I had to keep all my snide comments to myself. Right as I was about to ask Grace if this was Lissi's late-night-show audition, Grace leaned over and whispered, "I'm so proud of you for the way you're handling this, for being the bigger person." How was I supposed to tell her I wasn't?

"This will be a whole weekend with my ex's girlfriend," I protested.

"Yeah, and you're with Spence now," she countered.

Terri stood up. "That's what this is really about, isn't it? Spence."

Grace looked taken aback. "Is it?"

"No," I said. Terri's eyes bored into mine. "Not entirely. I mean, I'll probably hang out with him. But that's not why I decided not to go. It's expensive, it's far, and I'm not a volleyball player this year." I wasn't going to tell them that Spence had agreed with me that going was ridiculous. He'd made decent points like why would I pay so much money to stay in a cabin in the cold with people I could see right here in Brooksvale for free? When he said it that way, it made perfect sense—although, seeing my friends' reactions, I wasn't so sure now. Spence said I'd still have a great weekend if I didn't go, that he'd make it special. The idea of something romantic seemed a lot more tempting than being stuck in a cabin with Lissi.

"Cam," Grace said, "come on. You're bummed you missed the dance and everything. How do you think you're going to feel when you miss a whole weekend?"

"For a *boy*," Terri added.

"It's not for him!" I shouted. "I don't want to go. Don't you realize how hard it would be for me to be there? To have to listen to Lissi talk about *Marc*?"

"So it's because of Marc? You can't let guys keep you from doing things," Terri said, refusing to look at me.

I didn't know why she cared so much; it wasn't like she was going to be on the trip. "They're not," I said. "This is my choice."

"Right," she mumbled loud enough so I could hear.

"I wish you'd change your mind, but okay," Grace said, accepting the fact that I wouldn't.

"I know." I looked at everyone in the room. No one seemed to know what to say. I'd made things super awkward. "But I'm here now, and don't we have a movie to watch?"

"Yeah." Avery held a bowl up in the air. "Everyone have enough popcorn? Anyone need a drink?"

While the rest of the group figured out the snack situation, I walked over to Terri. "Why are you so upset?"

"You're just doing it again," she said.

"Doing what?"

She waved me off. "Forget it."

"No, tell me."

"Fine—you're letting a guy dictate your life."

I let out a sigh. "It's not like that. Come on, would you want to be jammed in a cabin with twenty girls? With one, maybe two bathrooms? And with someone you really wanted to avoid?"

I think I hammered the point home, because her shoulders relaxed. "Okay," she said, "let's go watch the movie."

We took seats on the couch, but Terri's words buzzed in my head. She was wrong. I was canceling the trip for me, not anyone else.

I was the one who decided what I wanted. Not Marc, not Spence—and not Terri, either. She might have been my best friend, but she didn't know what she was talking about.

Chapter 27

> **GRACE**
> Last chance! We're about to leave.

I felt a twinge of guilt as I read Grace's text. I knew I'd have a better time staying in Brooksvale, but I was sad I'd be missing out on team bonding. Even with Lissi there, I did have a lot of fun on the court cheering everyone on.

I was making the right decision, I assured myself as I texted her back.

> Have a great time!! We'll do something when you get back, and you can tell me all about it!!! ♡♡

I put away my phone and headed to the car. My parents were letting me drive to Spence's. I wrapped my arms around myself, the crisp air sending a chill through me. *You wanted this.*

What was my problem? I'd been looking forward to this weekend. I needed to snap out of it. I shook out my arms and got in the car. I was done being ridiculous. I was going to see Spence and everything was going to be amazing.

He greeted me with a kiss, and I couldn't help but grin up at him. It wasn't like butterflies were performing Cirque du Soleil in my stomach or anything, but it made me feel nice, comfortable, and it gave me hope for the future. Butterflies would come later. Maybe even this weekend. We—okay, technically me—were planning all sorts of romance-filled things to do.

I pulled him in for a longer kiss, hoping to set the tone, which got no protests from Spence. He wrapped his arms tighter around me, and I was pretty sure I even felt my stomach flip a little.

I forced myself to step back. "Your parents are here." Both their cars were parked in the driveway.

He gave me a light peck on the lips. "I think they know I kiss my girlfriend."

Girlfriend. I really liked that word.

"I'm not taking any chances. Come on," I said, tugging his hand. "The prelude to romance weekend is about to get underway."

He led me to the basement, where he picked up the remote control, did a bow with extra flourish, and presented it to me. "M'lady."

Tonight there were going to be no superheroes; it was all rom-coms. "Thank you," I said, taking it from him.

I tried not to show my disappointment as I sat down on the couch and looked around the room. I knew tonight was going to be the low-key portion of our weekend, but I'd still hoped for something a little extra. Not necessarily candles and rose petals all around the room—I didn't want any fire hazards or for his parents to flip out—but maybe some twinkly lights, a bouquet of flowers, a box of candy, a card with a dancing milkshake on it . . . something. Anything to show that Spence got me. But maybe he'd surprise me with all of that tomorrow.

"Okay, what's it going to be?" I asked, shaking off any lingering letdown. "Did you look at the movie choices I sent you?"

He put his arm around me. "Any of them are fine."

"Yeah, but which one spoke to you?"

Spence laughed. "Spoke to me?"

"Yes." I swatted his arm. "Did any of them stand out?" I'd crafted a list of movies for him to choose from, ranging from the eighties until now. It included some of my favorites, like *Say Anything*, *Ten Things I Hate About You*, *To All the Boys I've Loved Before*, and about a dozen more.

"I mean, they all seemed about the same."

"The *same*?!"

"I'm sorry. They're not really my thing, but I'm fine watching whichever one."

He must have seen my expression, because he quickly spoke again. "The second one you said—that one sounds good."

I let out a sigh. I was being stupid. It didn't matter that he didn't like rom-coms; my friends weren't the biggest fans, either, but they watched them anyway for me. And that was what Spence was doing. It was a good thing.

"Nice choice," I told him, and then pulled out a container of chocolate-covered strawberries from my bag. "I made these for us. But we can't eat them all tonight. We have to save some for tomorrow."

Tomorrow was going to be perfect. We were going to go apple picking, and then have a little autumn picnic in Brooksvale Park. I knew this cute little patch of grass that overlooked the town next door and would give us a perfect view of the sunset. It was supposed to be a clear night, too, so after, we could snuggle close to each other, wrapped in a big blanket, and gaze up at the stars and talk about our wishes. I couldn't wait.

"About that . . . ," he said, moving his arm away and turning to face me.

The words made me freeze. I knew I wasn't going to like this.

Spence bowed his head and looked up through his lashes. "Maybe we can postpone?"

"What? Why?"

"It's a good reason. Promise. It's about my brother. Duke called a little while ago—he was an alternate for this big e-sports tournament, and he found out he's going to get to play."

An alternate? For e-sports? What? Someone got a finger sprain or something and now my plans were ruined? It wasn't fair. "You see him play all the time. This weekend was supposed to be for us."

He gave me a sheepish smile. "I know, I'm sorry, but this is a big deal. And you can come! I want you to come. You've never seen Duke play. He's amazing. And you'll love this. There's this party for the gamers, and I actually want to go."

"You hate parties."

"I know, right? But Duke wants to show me around and introduce me to people. It'll be great for networking. Tournament organizers and other players will be there. Double win—you love parties. It'll be fun."

I didn't know what to say. Did Mr. Anti-Social really think this was a good thing? "You wouldn't stop by the dance or anywhere I wanted to go, not even for a minute, but you're ready to drop everything for this?"

Spence raked his hand through his hair. "This isn't like a normal party. You get that, right?"

Yeah, it was a party that interested him, while none of mine did.

When I didn't answer, he squeezed my knee. "I'll make it up to you. We'll do all the stuff you had planned another weekend. It's not like the apples are going anywhere."

"Actually," I spat, "they are. It's getting cold. It's going to frost soon. This could be the last weekend."

"Okay, then we'll just go when they grow back."

When they grow back? That wouldn't be until next year. My stomach was definitely turning now. Only it wasn't from butterflies; it was from dread. Why was the thought of still being with Spence a year from now making me feel this way? I liked him, right?

Of course I did.

I was just angry.

"Cam?" Spence said. "Say something."

"I gave up stuff for you. Stuff I wanted to go to."

Now he looked taken aback. "I never stopped you from going anywhere."

"Spence!" He might not have told me not to, but his expressions certainly had.

"What?"

"I gave up the volleyball trip. You're the one who convinced me to stay, told me we'd hang out, do fun stuff, and now you're bailing."

He laughed incredulously. "You didn't stay for me. *You* said you couldn't stand Lissi. *You* said it was expensive, and cramped, and I don't know."

I wrung my hand around my wrist. "Okay, whatever. That's not the point. *We* made plans, and I made my decision based on that."

He threw his hands up. "This thing with Duke just came up. It wasn't like I was keeping it a secret. And I'm not bailing; I'm including you. You like video games. It's not like I'm asking you to go somewhere tedious."

"Think again," I snapped. "Playing the games is bad enough. Watching them? Ten times worse."

Spence's eyebrows scrunched together. "What?"

"Come on," I said, lowering my voice, "you know I only play because you want to."

He shook his head. "I thought you liked it. I knew you hadn't played much before, but you always seemed up for it. You even came to one of my games."

I bit my lip. He wasn't wrong. I'd never said anything to him.

Spence ran his fingers through his hair again. "I guess I can tell my brother I can't make it."

He was going to give up something he really cared about because of me. Except that I didn't want him to.

I'd made that mistake enough for the both of us. I gave up my trip. I skipped the school dance, parties, and nights out with friends. I watched movies I didn't want to see, made myself available when he needed help with homework or studying. I even went to an e-tournament he played in.

Oh my God.

The sense of dread was back. My stomach felt heavy. I'd given up what I wanted to do for what I thought my boyfriend wanted.

Terri was right. I'd let a guy take over my life.

I looked at Spence.

"What?" he asked. "What's wrong?"

I'm sure my eyes bugged out, because it was like I was really seeing him for the first time. Spence was great, I liked spending time with him, but a realization was bubbling to the surface. I liked spending time with my friends a lot more. I had wanted a boyfriend so bad that I'd convinced myself Spence was perfect for me, but he wasn't. Not even close. I was forcing it. Worse, I had given up the things I loved for the things he loved. I'd chosen him over me, and I was done.

"Spence, you should spend the weekend with your brother."

"You'll come?"

I shook my head.

His body got stiff. "You're breaking up with me, aren't you?"

"I'm sorry."

I felt a flood of relief.

"But—" he started.

I cut him off. I didn't want him to try to convince me to change my mind. It was set. "Spence, I want to do all these things you never want to do."

"I never stopped you."

He was right. He hadn't—I'd stopped myself, because I wanted to be there for him. "I know, but I put you first. I did whatever you wanted to do, but you wouldn't even try the things I wanted."

Spence shook his head. "So you're blaming me for missing out on stuff?"

"No, I'm blaming *me*. I haven't stood up for myself, for what I've wanted, but that has to change. It's changing now."

We talked a little more before we said our goodbyes. It was awkward, but it was what I had wanted Marc to do for me, and I owed that to Spence. I owed that to myself. I think Spence understood where I was coming from. We left on decent terms, but I was excited that we were over. Excited to be done with Spence, done with doing things for other people.

It was time for me to do things for *me*.

Chapter 28

Terri's lips were attached to Chris Tanaka's when I found her outside the track Monday after school. I leaned against the fence and waited. Chris was our year, and he and I had a few classes together. I gave Terri and Chris a few minutes, but when they showed no signs of separating, I cleared my throat. Loudly.

She gave me a little wave and said goodbye to Chris. "See you tonight," she told him before he headed for his car, and we headed for the track.

"Is that why you wanted to meet here?" I asked her as we started our first loop around the course.

"No, that was just a bonus. Ran into Chris on the way out of school, and one thing led to another. We made a date." Her voice was singsongy.

"Do you even know Chris?" I asked her.

"I do now," she said, raising her eyebrows up and down. "We've been flirting in English the last couple of weeks," she admitted.

I didn't bother to ask if this had relationship potential. No guy lasted long with Terri. "But that's beside the point," she said. "I picked here so you can find someone, too."

"I thought you were happy to have me back and not spending

all my time with a guy." Right after the breakup, I'd filled her in on what went down with Spence. She was so happy, you'd have thought I told her I'd won the lottery.

"I am happy to have you back," she said. "But you know my issue wasn't about you spending time with someone else, right? Not that you should be spending *all* of your time with anyone. I just think whoever you go out with, it needs to be on your terms. You need to be happy. You need to get something out of it."

We started rounding the track.

"So let me get this straight," I said. "You want me to find a new boyfriend?"

"*No.* I want you to find a date. Someone to hang out with, *not* someone to plan the rest of your year with, or follow around like a puppy dog. Dating is fun."

"Maybe . . ."

"No maybe," she said, "definitely."

"If I concede that, will you concede that if you date the *right* person, getting into a relationship can be a good thing, too?"

She hemmed a moment. "For people older than us? Sure."

"Terri! It can work now, too. Grace's parents met in high school."

She held up a finger. "Exception, not the rule."

I threw my head back. "Relationships can be good things, when they're the right ones."

"You're not going to know what's right until you figure out what *you* like."

She could be exasperating at times. "And what does the track have to do with any of this?" I asked, power walking to keep up with her stride.

"You can't date unless you have someone to do it with." Terri gestured around us. "I brought you to the boys."

She had to be kidding. "At the *track*? You do remember it's Grace who gets up every morning to work out, not me, right? I'm not the exercise buff here."

"Yes, but since *someone*," she said, giving me the side-eye, "doesn't want to go to the mall anymore since the guy she just dumped works there, and it's two thirty in the afternoon on a school day, I couldn't think of anywhere else to go."

"So what am I supposed to do?" I asked, lowering my voice as three guys on the track team passed us on the left. "Chase them down? I swear, I don't know how you meet so many guys. This is impossible."

"No it's not. They're just people. You say hello. You talk. That's it. I do it at parties and things all the time. You just have to get over your fear. Be the out-there-in-your-face girl you used to be."

"I don't know," I said, taking in a deep breath. "Are you working on your art school applications?" I asked, changing the subject before she egged me on to go talk to a stranger or something.

"Yes, but I don't know what the point is; my parents aren't going to let me go."

"You leave that to Grace, Luke, and me," I told her. "The Tuesday after Halloween your parents will be completely swayed into sending you wherever you want to go."

Terri's mouth quirked. "What are you planning?"

"Not telling," I said, huffing slightly, as we began another lap.

"You're really not going to say? Not even a clue?"

"I'm really not, and I made the others swear to keep their mouths shut, too. So quit trying to pry something out of them."

She shook her head at me. "*Anyway*," she said, "how's the yearbook coming along?"

"There is so much work."

"You have Lissi."

I threw my head back. "Don't remind me. I emailed her some stuff to work on. I'm trying to avoid face-to-face contact at all costs."

Terri elbowed me lightly. "You got this, and I'm still on board to design the cover and hand-draw all the page headers. Hopefully, that will help."

"It will. You're great." Her lettering work was beautiful. "And I appreciate it."

"It'll be fun," she said. "And the college applications. How are they?"

I let out a sigh. "I'm still bummed I can't apply early decision to Columbia." I needed to wait so I could beef up my extracurricular activities and show off my senior-year grades. "But my application is looking pretty solid to me. I just hope they see it the same way. If I'm not in New York next year, I'm going to lose it."

"There're a lot of schools in New York, you know," she said.

"Yeah, but Columbia is my dream."

"Marc's," she mumbled under her breath, but I caught it.

"*And* mine." This wasn't like going to soccer games or watching superhero movies. New York was something I'd wanted even before I noticed boys. My aunt took me there for my birthday when I was ten. We saw a Broadway show, went shopping, ate sooo much food. The trip made me fall in love with the city.

"Look, I'm not trying to give you a hard time," she said, her voice soft. "It's just, have you even visited the school? You keep saying how much you love New York and that's why you want to be there, but Columbia is like its own little campus. It's not even in the parts of the city you're constantly raving about."

"But I can get there. It's not like Connecticut. New York has tons of ways to get around that don't involve owning a car."

"I know, and I'm not saying you shouldn't go to Columbia. I'm just saying you should see what else is out there. You've had this idea since freshman year that you needed to go to this particular school, but it doesn't mean there's not something better."

I sucked in my cheeks. Columbia was incredible. Marc and I had spent hours talking about it and looking over the website. I even slept in T-shirts from the school. It had everything, but I hated to admit that Terri may have had a point. There was a chance I hadn't really looked into the other schools in the area.

"If we're just going to talk about college," I said, pivoting back to our initial conversation and away from one I was over, "could we at least do it over fries at Scobell's, not on a track?"

"Your Scobell's ban didn't last long."

"I already went with the volleyball team, and you can only pass up their shakes for so long. But I'm standing by my decree to never have another date there."

"Third time's the charm."

"I doubt that."

"Okay," she said, "noted. Let's find you someone to take some-place other than Scobell's."

"Really?"

"Did you think I forgot the reason for bringing us to the track?" Terri asked. "Come on, we're here—you might as well make the most of it. Plenty of hot guys have passed us. Pick one."

"They're running! I can't keep up," I objected.

"They stop; they take breaks. Look, there's one at three o'clock, sitting on the bench, tying his shoes. Go get him. You got this. Go!"

The way she said it, the way she was pumping me up, just struck me as funny. It reminded me of when we played *Rocky* when we were younger. Grace, Terri, and I first watched the movie when it popped up on TV one Saturday in fifth grade. For about a year afterward, every time we'd go upstairs or had to run somewhere, we'd pretend we were Rocky training for his big fight. "The world ain't all sunshine and rainbows," I quoted from the film.

She didn't miss a beat. "Go out and get what you're worth," she quoted back.

Before I knew it, I found myself running in slow motion while humming the *Rocky* theme.

"What are you doing?" she asked, laughing.

I put my arms in the air in the victory sign and continued on my slow sprint. "Beating you around the track."

The next thing I knew she was next to me, and we were neck and neck in a snail's-pace race.

When we made it to the other side, where the guy was now standing, I slow-moed my way to victory. "Chaaaampiooooooon," I said, dragging out the word and jumping up and down in exaggerated, sluggish movements, while Terri languidly fell to the ground in defeat.

We attracted a little crowd. We should have been embarrassed, but we weren't. We were totally amusing ourselves, and apparently a few others, too. The hot guy and some people in the vicinity applauded. I bowed. "Thank you all very much." I extended my arm to Terri, who curtsied.

Feeling particularly emboldened by my little stunt, I walked over to Mr. Hottie. "Think I earned a place on the track team?"

"Indoor track is taking sign-ups," he said.

"Are you on the team?" I asked. I channeled my inner Terri and gave him a big smile and maintained eye contact.

"I am," he said.

Make Terri proud, I told myself, and upped my flirting game. "Then maybe I *should* sign up." I winked.

"Yeah," he said, and nodded. "We could use more people. My girlfriend would love having another female on the team."

Girlfriend?!

Oh God. *Awkward*. Was it okay for me to sprint away? We *were* on a track. My gut was churning, but instead of from fear, it was from laughter building up inside me. Of course he'd have a girlfriend. Why would I think anything would go right when it came to my love life?

"Nice," I said, not knowing what else to say, "I'll get right on that." I gave him a thumbs-up and pointed in front of me. "Got another race to finish." Then I went back into slow-motion-sprinting mode and headed straight to the parking lot. I kept it up all the way there, Terri once again my faithful running partner.

When we got to her car, we both doubled over with laughter.

"That," she said through her giggling fit, "was awesome."

"OhmyGodohmyGodohmyGod." I couldn't control my breath. "All that, and he had a girlfriend."

"I know," she said, gasping herself. "That's what made it even better. The look on your face, and then you started that pantomime running."

She waved her hands, trying to calm herself down, but she wound up in another laughing fit, which only made me laugh harder.

"What's so funny?" someone shouted at us from afar.

"We are!" I yelled back, causing Terri to snort-laugh.

"Look," she said when we finally got some of our composure back, "this was good—you put yourself out there. So what if you didn't wind up with the guy? It will make the next time you try to talk to someone even easier. And think about the story you have now. Grace is going to crack up when you tell her."

"What came over me?" I asked, getting into her car.

"Maybe a sense of fun?" she said, putting the key in the ignition. "I missed this side of you."

"What are you talking about?" I put on a fake pout. "I'm always fun."

She turned to face me. "Yeah, but you used to do things like this all the time. Remember the eighth-grade dance, when you pulled Grace and me onstage during that Kevin Wayward song and made us do that bizarre interpretive dance? Or the talent show in seventh, where you had us perform dramatic readings of kid songs?"

I laughed. "I still stand by that. It was epic. Row, row," I said in my most serious voice, "row your boat." I paused for five seconds. "Gently. Down the stream."

"Yes," she said, "it was. We always did stuff like that, usually because of you, and then when we started high school, and you started seeing Marc, it stopped."

"It didn't stop."

"It kind of did," she said.

"Hey," I objected. "We've reenacted those dramatic readings millions of times. You're usually the one who refuses."

"Yeah, you, me, and Grace have done a lot of stuff, stuff I usually put up a stink about, but it's always in private. Until the whole Brooksy thing, the only time I've seen you do something even a little wild in public was when you'd cheer at one of Marc's or Grace's games. And even that was fairly tame."

Was she right? I mean, we didn't have a talent show in the high school for me to take part in, even if I'd wanted to. But we did have dances . . . and I never jumped onstage or did anything showy there.

It totally would have embarrassed Marc. He was more subdued, but he'd never told me to tone it down. I just did.

I guess I had done a lot of things for Marc, but I hadn't completely given up things I liked. Had I?

If I was honest, I knew the answer, because I'd just done the same thing with Spence.

I didn't even give anyone the chance to know the real me. I hid myself, hoping it would make me seem like a better choice. The thought made me cringe.

Well, I was not doing that anymore.

From here on out, I was going to work on finding the old Cam, the real Cam. The Cam who did outlandish dances and ridiculous performances and didn't care what anyone thought. The Cam who had fun and knew what she wanted.

I hadn't known she'd disappeared, but now that I did, I was realizing just how much I missed her. And I was going to do everything I could to get her back.

Chapter 29

"I think I may need a live reenactment of that," Avery said the next day at lunch after I shared my track story.

"Forget that," Nikki interrupted. "Can we get back to this whole you dumping Spence thing? I've been thinking about it all night, and I'm still kind of in shock here."

I told them everything about the breakup yesterday. I didn't think it'd be possible for Nikki to have any more questions. She'd already asked me a gazillion. But apparently I was wrong.

Avery elbowed her.

"What?" Nikki protested, tossing a chip in her mouth. "It was all Spence this, Spence that, and then, snap, just like that, no warning, he's gone."

"I think it's good," Meg said.

"Yeah," Naamua agreed. "No offense, Cam, but you guys didn't seem to have that much in common."

"No offense taken. He was a good guy, but you're right, he wasn't for me."

All four of my lunchtime crew—Avery, Nikki, Meg, and Naamua—nodded. If you had told me a year ago I'd be hanging out with a group of cheerleaders every day, I wouldn't have believed it. But somehow, over a fairly short period of time, the four of them had turned into good friends.

"So who *is* right for you?" Nikki asked, raising her eyebrows up and down.

"No clue." I took a bite of my turkey sandwich. "That's the million-dollar question."

"I bet we can come up with someone," she said, and made a little circle motion with her finger at the rest of my friends at the table.

Was she serious? "I don't know, Nikki."

"Well, I do. We know *so* many people. It wouldn't be hard. Let us play matchmaker."

Before I could even think about objecting, Nikki had her phone out and punched up GroupIt. "Okay, Naamua, you're up first. Ooh. There are some hotties on your friends list that I don't know. Holding out on us, huh? All right, let's see here. Cam's future boyfriend. What about Andre Paiva, Kel Wala, or Tony Benedetto?"

"Nope, nope, and nope," Naamua said. She put up three fingers and lowered them one by one as she ticked off her reasons. "Incredibly old picture—he's a friend of the family who's like forty; lives in LA; has a girlfriend."

"Okay," Nikki said, looking back at her phone. "Alberto Medina, what about him? He's really cute, too."

"Yeah, and I'm sure his boyfriend agrees with you," Naamua said.

"Maybe it would be better if we went through our own lists," Meg offered. "Would probably save a lot of time if we each picked someone we knew ourselves."

Nikki stood up.

"What? What's wrong?" I asked.

"I just had an amazing idea," Nikki whisper-shouted.

Avery tugged at her arm. "Why don't you sit back down and tell us about it?"

"Okay. You know *The Bachelorette*? I *love* that show. We do our own version starring Cam. There's the bonfire in the park this Friday. We each bring a guy, and Cam can pick who she likes the best. Four dates, one night." Nikki was bouncing in her seat. She turned to me. "You can even bring a rose and give it to your favorite suitor."

"Nikki!"

"What?" she asked incredulously.

"This is my life, not a reality show," I said.

"Why can't it be both?"

I turned to the others for help. Meg shrugged.

"I don't know," Naamua said.

"What's not to know?" Nikki asked.

"Like, maybe the guys will be annoyed that we're trying to fix them all up with the same girl," Avery said, being the voice of reason.

"Oh please, it's going to be at a party. If Cam doesn't like them, or they don't like her—no offense, Cam—they move on, meet someone new. Think about it, what guy our age wants a blind date anyway? They'll like this better. We'll just mention we have someone they should talk to. It's not like we're going to tell them a bunch of people are trying to fix Cam up."

"Or we could—a little competition might be fun," Meg said.

Nikki nodded. "Now you're talking."

"No," I said, vetoing that idea. "If we do this, and I repeat *if*, we don't mention the other guys."

"This is sounding like a yes," Nikki said in a happy singsong voice.

I squeezed my wrist. "I don't know."

"We *need* to do this," Nikki pressed. "These parties are all the same. Let's spice things up a little . . . and help your love life," she added. "Come on, come on, come on."

I looked to Avery.

"Well," she said, bobbing her head back and forth, "it could work. I mean, you're supposed to talk to a bunch of different people at parties anyway—so what if they're planned, right? It will be efficient, and it could be pretty amusing. I guess it's not the worst idea I've ever heard."

"It's a *brilliant* idea," Nikki stressed again. "Be our Bachelorette."

I thought about what Terri had said the other day.

The old Cam wouldn't have said no, I reminded myself. She would have cracked up over the idea and immediately jumped on board.

"Okay," I told Nikki, "count me in."

Chapter 30

"We're here," Grace said as Terri pulled the car into a spot at one of the parking lots at Brooksvale Park.

Tonight's bonfire was being held by the lake on the north side of the park. There was a pavilion and a little raised stage where a student band was going to perform. Normally the area was off-limits at night in the fall, but an exception had been made for tonight. The bonfire was a Brooksvale High tradition that had been going on forever.

The three of us got out. "You know, Cam," Terri said, looking me over, "I like the red sweater dress and all, but I really think you should be wearing a ball gown. You know, seeing as you're the new Bachelorette."

"Who knew you were so funny," I deadpanned, but she knew I was kidding. The whole idea of a mass setup was absurd, but it was also oddly intriguing, and they thought so, too.

For my outfit I'd gone with the aforementioned sweater dress, leggings, chunky boots, and a little jacket. Appropriate for the elements, yet still cute.

Terri rounded the car toward me. "Maybe I'm just jealous of all the attention you're going to get."

"*You?*" I elbowed her playfully. "I'll bet you twenty bucks you'll have some guy hanging all over you within the hour." As predicted, Chris was ancient history. Terri had long forgotten him even though it hadn't even been a full week.

She winked at me. "No way. I can't afford to give away money like that, but don't worry, you will have my utmost attention tonight. I need a front-row seat for this dating show you've got going on."

"Me too"—Grace jumped in—"and I'll keep my eyes open for any interesting prospects at the bonfire. Maybe I can enter a contestant, too!"

We neared the pavilion. "Forget me," I said. "We need to find someone for you."

"No." Grace had a look of warning in her eyes. "We don't."

I held up my hands. "Fine, I won't play matchmaker." I raised my eyebrows up and down. "Tonight. But be prepared: Halloween's a whole other story." We had Gretchen Haskin's party that night.

"Are you trying to convince me not to go?" she asked.

"Not possible," Terri said.

"Yeah," I agreed. "You love Halloween way too much to miss it."

It was her favorite holiday. Every year she made us dress up in some sort of group costume. This time we were going as the Chipmunks. I was Alvin, Grace was Simon, and Terri was Theodore. I preferred cuter outfits, but Grace was always adamant that we go as a trio, and she was persistent. It's how I ended up as a Sanderson sister from *Hocus Pocus* last year, scissors from rock-paper-scissors the year before that, and Snap from the Snap, Crackle, Pop Rice Krispies elves the one before that.

"Fine, maybe," she relented. "But when else do you get to dress up in ridiculous outfits in public?"

"Look who you're talking to," I reminded her. "Try every volleyball game." Then I threw in my badger cry for good measure.

"Keep making that sound," Terri said. "I hear guys love that; they'll be fighting over you."

"It brought me over," Luke said, approaching us, Paisley's arm linked with his.

The five of us headed to the pavilion to get a drink, weaving our way through a huge crowd of students. While the bonfire wasn't officially a school-sponsored event, it had school approval. A bunch of parents and local restaurants and shops even supplied food, sodas, and punch—although some people snuck in things a little stronger.

"There you are!" Nikki yelled from about twenty feet away. "We've been looking for you."

She said *we* but was alone when she approached.

"Where's everyone else?" I asked.

Nikki looked at me like I was dense. "Getting your suitors ready for the big reveal." A rose was sticking out of her purse. She noticed me looking at it. "This," she said, presenting the flower to me like it was a sacred scepter, "is for you."

"I am not giving that out."

"Sure you are. It's part of the fun." Nikki put the rose behind my ear. "Now let's meet Bachelor Number One." She texted someone, and a few minutes later Miles Coffield was standing in front of me.

"Oh," he said, his whole body stiffening.

I crossed my arms over my chest. This wasn't going to go well.

"*Cam's* the one you wanted me to meet? Yeah, I don't think so."

"What?" Nikki asked, her excitement fizzling like a balloon with a hole in it as Miles shook his head and walked away.

"Rejection at its finest," I said.

Paisley tugged at Luke's arm. She looked uncomfortable. *We should go*, she mouthed. I think she was trying to be subtle, but I saw it anyway.

"We're going to go dance," Luke said, taking a step away from me. The two of them were trying to spare me some embarrassment, but it was too late. Bachelor Number One had already seen me and made a run for it in front of everyone. "Have fun," I said.

"I don't get it. Why would he do that?" Nikki complained. "Miles is not that rude, and he was supposed to be the winner. Cute, sports fan but not a player, funny, our year. Will somebody please tell me what just happened here?"

"He hates her," Terri offered.

"Obviously," Nikki said. "Why?"

Terri snorted. "He may hold a tiny bit of resentment toward her. He wound up in summer school because of Cam."

"It's his fault," I clarified. "Miles was in my social studies class freshman year and was constantly trying to cheat off me. During the final, I had enough. I yelled, 'Stop looking at my paper!' I hadn't meant to scream, I was just annoyed, but it got the teacher's attention. Miles flunked the test, needed to repeat the course over the summer, and blamed me."

"And now, a few years later, it's coming back to bite *me*." Nikki downed her drink. "I can't believe my guy is out of the running already. You couldn't have told me this before?"

"How was I supposed to know you would pick Miles? You should have told him my name ahead of time. Or vice versa. The show does."

She cocked her head and gave me a stare. "I was trying to keep it mysterious, like old-school *The Bachelorette*. The bachelors used to get out of a limo and meet the Bachelorette for the first time. The guys were always relieved to see who the mystery woman was. It always worked there."

Nikki made some sort of raspberry sound with her lips and started texting again. "I hate losing. I guess it is what it is. Don't worry, though," she said, I think reassuring herself more than me, "I'm still on board for the rest of the competition. I told the others where we are, and to start bringing over the suitors." She let out a sigh. "Any other guys we need to stay clear of?"

"Probably tons," Terri answered for me, and I swatted her arm.

"Ooh," Nikki said, switching from disappointment to hope in the bat of an eyelash. "Who's Grace talking to? Derrick somebody, right? He could be a possibility."

We all turned to see. Grace was at the other end of the table, chatting up a storm. She must have felt our eyes on her, because she looked up and immediately came back over.

I eyed her suspiciously. "What's going on with you two?" This wasn't the first time I'd caught them together.

"Nothing," she said. "I just thought he might know someone for you."

I would take all the help I could get, and apparently Nikki agreed.

"Good," she said, nodding in approval. "We need as many contestants as we can find. My guy is out, which sucks, but on the upside it means I can be an unbiased judge. We're going to find Cam's perfect match. Just think of me as the producer, perusing all the guys in Brooksvale, testing them and narrowing the field of suitors down until Cam chooses the perfect guy."

"Excuse me?"

It was Anthony Fazzini. He had just walked over with Naamua.

"This is some sort of contest for Cam?" He turned to Naamua. "Why would you do this?"

When she didn't answer—she looked like she didn't know what to say; I mean, how do you explain you're part of a high school version of *The Bachelorette*?—he got annoyed and stalked off, but not before ruining my chances with the next guy.

"You might want to stay away from her," Anthony told Cooper Matthews, who was walking up with Avery. "Bet they're trying to get you to 'talk' to Cam, too, huh?" He scoffed. "FYI, they're just trying to mess with us."

"No we're not," I protested.

"Whatever," Anthony said, and kept his focus on Cooper. "If you want to be a part of their joke, that's on you."

Cooper looked around at all of us standing there, me with a rose behind my ear. "This doesn't look fishy or anything," he mumbled. Then he said, "Sorry, Avery. I don't know what's going on here, but there are a ton of girls to talk to at this thing; I don't need this."

Then the two guys walked off together. Two really good options, gone. My friends had done a great job in their casting of bachelors. Both guys had always seemed super nice. I'd never heard anyone say anything bad about either of them. Cooper was on the chess team, a swimmer, and totally hot. And Anthony was just as good-looking. He was in the marching band and the peer advocates—a volunteer group that spoke with students reaching out for help. Most important, they'd known that it was me they were being set up with, and they may have been interested until they found out about each other. My Mr. Perfect could have been either of them, and now neither wanted anything to do with me. I was quickly regretting this *Bachelorette*-style approach to dating.

"Sorry," Nikki said, "for my big mouth. I should have spaced these meetings better."

"It's not your fault," I said. "I think maybe we should leave reality TV to the professionals. It's time to call it quits."

"Without meeting Grayson?" Meg asked, approaching with some guy I assumed was him.

Guys were creeping up like roaches all of a sudden. Normally this would have been a good thing—but not when they were scaring one another away.

"Relax," she told me, "he knows everything about the competition."

I wasn't sure he was so thrilled about being there. He was standing with his hands in his pockets, shuffling his feet.

"You don't think this is strange?" I asked.

He smiled. "Maybe a little," he said, peeking at me but not making full eye contact, "but I come from a family of *Bachelor* lovers, so how could I say no?"

Aw, he wasn't looking for an escape route. He was just shy, in an adorable way, and I was here for it.

Meg pulled him closer to me. "Cam, I wanted to introduce you to Grayson. He's my cousin's best friend. They go to the Academy." The Academy was the private school in town.

"Nice to meet you," I said. I was about to shake his hand, but then he wiped his nose with it, so I gave a little wave instead.

"How about we let them talk?" Meg said to my entourage, gesturing for them to follow her.

Grace gave me a thumbs-up. *This could be it*, she mouthed, looking more excited than even Nikki. Then they all headed for the dance floor, leaving me alone with Grayson.

Part of me wanted to join them—the music was really good, and I hadn't danced in forever—but I brought my attention back to my "suitor." I had to get my priorities straight. The goal of tonight was to find a guy. Not to party with my friends. Grayson could be the one I was looking for.

"The Academy, huh?" I asked, turning my attention to him. "I don't know, does that make us rivals?"

"I'm not into the rivalry thing," he said, and wiped his nose again. "Unless I'm playing, I don't go to any of the games. I don't care who wins."

"I was just joking."

"Oh, ha!"

"So you play a sport?" I asked.

"I'm on the basketball team, but there's way too many of us. So I'm basically on standby every other week."

"Do you go to the games when you're not playing?"

Grayson shook his head. "Nah, what's the point?"

I couldn't imagine not cheering on your own team. I hadn't even been on the volleyball team for the past couple of years, but I still showed up whenever I could to root Grace and the rest of them on.

"You on a team?" he asked, pushing his hands deeper into his pockets.

"Just the mascot," I said. "You know, the one who jumps around in a costume." It was hard not to look over at my friends. From where I was standing, I had a perfect view of everyone. They were in a giant group. Grace, Terri, Luke, Derrick, and Paisley were there, but so were Avery, Nikki, and a bunch of the cheerleading squad. They were all dancing together. No one seemed coupled up, or like they wished they were somewhere else. They were all just having fun.

"We can go dance with everyone," I suggested.

"I don't dance," Grayson said.

"How come?" I asked.

"Just don't like it." He wiped his nose again with the back of his hand. I wasn't sure if it was allergies or a nervous tic, but either way, it was kind of gross. Especially when there was a whole slew of napkins about five feet away from us on the table.

"Okay, um, what do you like to do?" I asked. It was a horribly generic question, one that I personally hated to be asked, but I was struggling for things to say.

"All sorts of things."

"Like . . . ," I pushed. This was getting more painful by the moment.

He answered, but I wasn't even listening, I couldn't stop watching my friends.

"What about you?" he asked.

Grace saw me, and she waved. I waved back.

"Same as you," I told him, scolding myself for losing track of why I was at the party in the first place. I needed to put effort into finding Mr. Right. Meg had set me up; the least I could do was have a little energy, make the guy feel comfortable opening up. Grayson had boyfriend potential. Getting distracted wasn't the way to win him over. I needed to pay better attention. "All sorts of things."

There was a pause; neither of us seemed to know what to say. "Ever been to a bonfire before?" I asked, grasping for something . . . anything.

"Nope."

I kicked a stick on the ground. "It's pretty cool."

"I guess we can go get a closer look," he said.

"Yeah, sure."

"Let's grab some food," Grayson suggested.

"Perfect."

Only was it?

Yes, it was, I told myself as I watched him pile his plate with chips, burgers, and pickles. This was going to be a good night. Grayson was nice. So what if he didn't want to dance? Or had no school spirit? Or a runny nose? He was a chance to have all the things I wanted in my senior year: a boyfriend to go with to parties and prom. A boyfriend to cuddle up with and talk to.

If that was what I wanted, why couldn't I stop glancing at my friends over my shoulder?

The band started blasting a cover of a Kevin Wayward song. The one about summer, and friendship, and fun. The one that had prompted me to pull Grace and Terri up onstage in middle school, where we did an interpretive dance. I bet Terri had requested this one.

"Oh no they're not," I whispered.

But they were. My friends were doing my moves. The swinging of the arms in a giant circle when the song mentioned the Ferris wheel, the extension of every limb to signify the sunset, the gyrating of their entire bodies to act like waves.

I couldn't believe they were doing the whole thing—especially without me there.

"Grayson," I said, "I'm so sorry, but I need to go dance. You can come."

He shook his head.

I'd offered, I had tried to include him, but I wasn't giving my night up for a guy I barely knew. Not again.

It was time that I learned from my mistakes.

I ran over to my friends, shaking my body like I was the water crashing onto the beach, matching Grace and Terri's moves. We were in sync. Pretty soon the others around us joined in, doing their own interpretations, each trying to top the others.

I couldn't stop laughing, especially when Grace went and lifted up Derrick, and he held out his arms like he was doing a pirouette. They definitely won for Ferris wheel impersonation.

"Someone's eyes are glued this way," Avery said, and nudged her chin in Marc's direction. He was standing by the drinks with Lissi, but he was staring at me.

I just rolled my eyes. I didn't care what Marc did. I had better things to do, like win an interpretive-dance contest. By the time the song ended, my whole group was in hysterics. I would have hated to have missed that. Especially over some guy.

I'd thought I wanted a boyfriend, but I was realizing that what I meant by that was someone who got me, who loved me despite—or maybe because of—my quirks. Someone who made me laugh, who I could talk with for hours, and who let me be me. And I already had someone like that—several someones, actually, and they were all right in front of me, jumping to the music.

Maybe I would find a boyfriend, my Mr. Perfect. But right now I had something better. I had my friends.

The band started playing another song, and Terri and Grace put their arms around me. We started spinning as fast as we could. I felt light-headed and free.

It was a feeling, a night, I would remember forever.

Chapter 31

"Woo-hoo," I screamed from the side of the auditorium. Avery and the rest of the cheerleaders cartwheeled to the center of the room. They were part of the pep rally leading up to homecoming weekend. All the fall sports teams were involved. The principal was calling them down team by team, where they would run over, do something corny with Brooksy—the official one, Sam Raucher, not me—get tons of applause, then take a seat in the first rows of bleachers.

It was supposed to bring about school spirit in time for homecoming weekend. Most of the teams had already played their final games for the season, but it didn't matter. Everyone was happy for a reason to get out of last period.

"I should not be going down there with you," I told Grace, who was up on her tiptoes, stretching out her calves.

"Um, yes, you should," she said. "You're part of the team."

"I ran around in a costume; you guys did the work. Especially you—you're the one who led them to victory. I lost track of all the points you scored." The team had won their championship game yesterday.

Grace put her hands on her hips. "A, your cheering helped

motivate us; you are totally a member of the volleyball team. You know that. And, B"—she gestured to the rest of the team members, who were standing near us—"it wasn't just me; the whole team got us the win."

She was being modest. "Yes, everyone was great," I admitted, "you all smoked your opponents, but just admit *you* were on fire."

A slow smile spread across her face. "I was good, wasn't I?"

"More than good."

"Cam," a fully costumed Sam called out to me as the cheerleaders moved to the bleachers and the cross-country team took center court. "Want to go be Brooksy?" he asked, taking off the badger head and dropping it at my feet.

I did, but I couldn't. "Can't have two Brooksys together. Cosmic ramifications. Possible spontaneous combustion. Or worse," I teased, "like having two Santa Clauses on the same Macy's parade float or two Mickey Mouses in the same area of Disney World, dashing hopes and dreams. It just isn't done. It's practically sacrilegious."

"You done?" he asked, giving me a blank stare, not seemingly amused by me at all.

He obviously wasn't in a joking mood. "Why do you want me out there?" I asked.

"Because," he said, shifting his weight onto his right side, "at the soccer game, I missed a landing on one on my backflips and twisted my ankle. I thought I was fine, but it's acting up. Will you finish up for me?"

There was no way I was passing this up. I'd thought I was done being Brooksy after the volleyball championship game. This was like my last hurrah. "Yeah, I gave back the costume, but it's probably just sitting in Coach's office. I can check."

He waved me off with his big furry paw. "There's not enough

time for that. Just use mine." He unzipped the back of his Brooksy costume and shimmied out of it.

I did *not* want to step into that thing. He had sweat all over it. The costumes were the cheap kind; we didn't have the air-conditioned ones they had at nice amusement parks. I didn't have time to debate the issue. The volleyball team was up next, and if I didn't want to miss it, it meant wearing Sam's costume.

It was time to suck it up. I got in the suit and picked up the head. *Gross, gross, gross.* I took a deep breath and placed it on top.

"And let's give it up for the Brooksvale volleyball team," the principal called out, right as I finished changing. "Reigning state champions!"

My concern over sweat, smell, and mustiness evaporated as I ran out with the team, arms pumping into the air. I may not have had the gymnastic ability of the previous Brooksy, but I had an unrivaled amount of enthusiasm.

I ran around the team once and then attempted cartwheels. Cartwheels, in the loosest sense of the word. It was more like moving around while hunched over, and kicking a leg in the air, but it didn't matter—the crowd was cheering.

I went over and tried to pick Grace up. I wanted to march her around the room, give her the full champion hurrah.

"Whoa, whoa, whoa," she said when I squatted and reached around her. "No way are you going to be able to do this. I have a better idea."

Before I knew it, I was in the air, with the team holding me up!

"Brooksy!" they yelled.

"Rawrr, rawrr, rawrr, rawrr," I said, bringing out my awful badger voice. "Go, Brooksvale!"

The whole team chanted with me.

When it was time for them to take their seats, they put me down so I could do my thing with the next group. I danced around, pretended to be in an imaginary match with the tennis team, putted around with the golf crew, and then it was time for soccer.

Marc and his team ran up, chanting "champions." They had won the championship for their division as well.

I didn't hesitate, I didn't think twice: I ran over and gave a high five to each of them. Even to Todd, who'd talked crap about me. Even to Vern, who'd gone from friend to pretending I didn't exist. Even to Marc, who'd broken my heart.

I was sick of being hurt, angry, and resentful. These guys were no longer my friends, but they didn't need to take up my energy, either.

I moved from them to the people on the bleachers, where I orchestrated a wave and another "Brooksvale" chant. Everyone took part, and I got that rush I'd come to love every time I was in front of a crowd.

The rest of the pep rally flew by. I took off my Brooksy head as the principal was making his closing remarks, reminding everyone to be safe this weekend, no drinking, texting and driving—or mischief, seeing that it was also Halloween.

I looked up at the stands, at the rows of classmates and friends—new and old—and I couldn't help but smile. The past couple of months had been full of surprises, not all wonderful, but, all things considered, senior year was shaping up to be a really good one.

Chapter 32

The bell rang after the pep rally, and everyone filed out, ready to start the weekend. As I headed to Coach's office to drop off Sam's Brooksy costume, I noticed Lissi leaning against the wall, looking over photos on her camera. She hadn't used her phone like most of us; she had an actual professional camera.

Since she'd joined yearbook, we hadn't spoken. All our communications had been through email, each of us working separately. I knew that needed to change. I took a deep breath. If I could be nice to Marc, I could be nice to Lissi. It was time to push history aside, or at least try to.

"Get any good shots?" I asked as I walked over to her.

"Cam!" She looked surprised that I was talking to her, which would have shocked no one. "Um, yeah. Here, look." She pulled up a photo and held out the camera. It was me moments ago at the rally, holding the Brooksy head and peering out at the crowd. It sounded corny, but I was seriously beaming. My smile was huge, and I looked like I could take on anything. "It's a great picture of you."

"You took this?" I asked her.

Lissi nodded. "I grabbed a bunch, thought I might get some usable ones for the yearbook." She swiped through about a dozen photos from the rally. "There's a lot more."

"These are really good," I said.

"Ya think?" She gave me a small, cautious smile.

"Yeah, I do."

"I took some at the bonfire, too. I made a yearbook mock-up page with some of the best ones, if you want to see it," she said.

I couldn't believe what I was about to say, but the words came out anyway. "That would be great. Maybe one day next week we can go over all the yearbook stuff together, pick some photos, and work on layout? I mean, if you want."

She nodded. "I do. I'd like that."

"Me too," I said, and the thing was—I think I actually meant it.

Chapter 33

"Thanks for the ride," I told my mom as I jumped out of the car at Gretchen Haskin's house for the Halloween party.

"Terri's giving you a ride home?" she asked.

"Yep," I assured her. My sister and I had decided to hit a few houses in our neighborhood for trick-or-treating before we each met up with our friends. I was really trying to make an effort to spend more time with Jemma, who was currently in the back seat wearing a Batman costume, popping a mini Snickers in her mouth.

"Don't eat all the candy," I warned her.

Jemma eyed my Alvin and the Chipmunks getup. "I'm saving your life. Chipmunks shouldn't eat chocolate. It's poison."

"I'll risk it," I told her.

"I'll try to save you some. No promises. I need my energy. I have a city to save."

I laughed. "Have fun tonight."

"You too."

I said my goodbyes and headed into Gretchen's to find my fellow rodents.

I couldn't find them, but I did spot Darth Vader, or rather Luke in a Darth Vader costume.

"Hey there," I said. "Everything still set for Tuesday?"

He put his hands in front of him, pretending to strangle something. "For the eighty-seventh time, yes. The room is set: Terri will have her art show."

"I know, I'm sorry." I'd been bugging him a lot about it. "I just still can't believe your aunt and uncle are letting us have it. It's a big ask. How'd you convince them?"

"I used the Force," he informed me, taking out his lightsaber and holding it in the air.

"Whatever works," I told him.

"Huh?" Terri asked, joining us, wrapping her arms around me. I squeezed her back.

"I sense something . . . ," Luke said, quoting a Vader line.

"Yeah, you sense the coolest Chipmunk in the house—no offense, Cam."

"None taken." I pointed to my costume. "I'm pretty sure Alvin is the cool one. But don't worry, Theodore tries hard."

"Do or do not," Luke said. "There is no try."

Terri looked at him like he was speaking Greek. "What?"

"He's quoting Star Wars," I explained to her.

"How do *you* know?" Terri asked.

I gave her the same look she had given Luke. "I don't *just* watch rom-coms. Besides, we all saw Star Wars together."

"Right. I sort of remember that," she said.

"But poor Luke here picked the wrong Jedi. What about your namesake?"

"Just wanted to emulate my father."

Terri groaned. "I don't know how much of this I'm going to be able to take."

Luke lifted his lightsaber again and tapped Terri on her shoulders like he was knighting her. "Give yourself to the Dark Side. It is the only way you can save your friends."

"I have officially entered Nerd Central," she said.

Luke put his saber back in his belt. "I don't know—I'm dressed as Darth Vader, and you're a Chipmunk. You may want to rethink the nerd-factor thing."

"He may have a point," I said.

Terri put her hands on her hips. "I'll have you know, our costumes are cool. You have to be confident to pull off an ugly-ass costume like this when everyone else is a sexy doctor, fireman, or even zombie."

She was right: Our costumes definitely didn't fall into the sexy category. They were black leggings with giant T-shirts over them. Terri's was a green one with a giant *T* on it (which she'd chosen for obvious reasons), Grace's was blue with a big *S*, and mine was red with a big *A*. Grace and Terri also had chipmunk ears, while I had a red cap. That was pretty much our entire getup, other than Grace's Simon glasses.

"Where's Paisley?" Terri asked.

"She and one of her friends are trying to get drinks," he said.

"Oooh, I want," she said. Terri gestured toward me. "Come on, she'll let us cut; we won't have to wait as long."

I shook my head. "You two go. I'm going to search for our missing chipmunk. I haven't seen Grace yet."

I circled the party a couple of times but I still couldn't find her, and she wasn't answering her texts.

As I checked my phone for the umpteenth time, I almost walked right into Avery. She was with Nikki and a cute guy. A *really* cute guy. He was five nine–ish, had gorgeous dark eyes, light brown skin, killer cheekbones, short dreads, and a tiny dimple when he smiled. He looked vaguely familiar, but I couldn't place from where.

"Sorry," I said to Avery, "I wasn't paying attention at all." I took in her costume. And Nikki's. "No! Really? You guys came as cheerleaders. This is your chance to dress up as anything, and you came as yourselves?"

"Right?" the guy agreed. "Major waste of Halloween."

"It's what happens when you wait until the last minute to figure out a costume," Avery informed us.

"But you're right," Nikki teased, "we're really missing out on the chance to be a cartoon rodent or . . ." She looked him over. "Who are you supposed to be again?"

"The Tenth Doctor."

"Whatever that means," Nikki said.

Avery laughed. "Someone's not a *Doctor Who* fan."

He slapped a hand over his heart. "You're killing me."

"Cam, this is my cousin Ty," she said.

"The cousin from the movie!?" I asked. That's why he looked familiar! He'd been in the Netflix movie Avery invited us over to see. She'd rewound and replayed the part he was in five times.

He lowered his head. "Guilty."

"What?" I asked. "You were good. She had us all over to watch."

"Avery, I had one line," Ty said. "You made them all sit through it?"

"Yes! It was a great movie," she declared, "and I'm your biggest fan. If you lived closer, I would have made you sit there while we watched it, too." Avery turned to me. "Ty's in town for my dad's fiftieth birthday tomorrow."

She patted his shoulder. "Sorry you had to give up a college party to be stuck back at a high school one."

"Oh, you're in college?" I asked. "Where do you go?"

"No," Nikki said, holding her hands up in the air, silencing us. "No college talk. I finally got my Princeton application done, by the skin of my teeth, and I do not want to think about school. Any school, at all. Not this weekend. I need a break. Pleeeeassse." Nikki was applying early action, and the deadline was tomorrow. She'd been majorly stressing out the past few days.

"Okay, okay," I said. "How about movies—is that okay?"

Nikki nodded. "Acceptable."

"Fine, will we be seeing you in anything else?" I asked Ty.

"Not on screen, but I am doing a musical at sch—the place that shall not be mentioned."

"Oh yeah? What show?"

"I'm in *Mary Poppins*."

"No way!" I shouted. "I love *Mary Poppins*. It was the first Broadway musical I ever saw. The only Broadway musical, actually. Who do you play?"

"Bert."

I may have let out a small gasp. "He's my favorite."

"Mine too."

"Chim chiminey, chim chiminey, chim chim cher-ee," I sang, channeling the chimney-sweep character.

"And that, my friends," Nikki announced, "is my cue to go get a drink."

I put my hands on my hips. "Are you saying my singing is scaring you away?"

She tapped the rim of my cap so that it covered my eyes. "That is exactly what I'm saying."

Avery took Ty's cup from him. "I'll get us refills. Want anything, Cam?"

I shook my head.

"Okay, we'll be right back." Nikki led her to the drinks table.

"My singing was not that bad," I protested once it was just me and Ty.

Ty winked. "I'm just glad you weren't at auditions—you would have beat me out for the part."

"I would've been stiff competition. Ya know, I've probably seen the original movie a hundred times."

"Don't tell anyone," he said, leaning closer and whispering, "but I've still never seen it."

"You what? No? No! You have to. Dick Van Dyke is amazing."

He laughed. It was a nice laugh—deep, throaty. "I know, I know, I know."

"Promise me you'll watch the movie. It's soooo good."

"Promise."

The familiar beat of Kevin Wayward started playing, and Terri hooted. I could see her arms raised in the air. I couldn't let her do our moves alone.

"Ty, it was really nice to meet you, but I have an interpretive dance to do."

I knew he probably had questions, but I didn't have time to answer them. I wasn't choosing a guy over my best friend.

"Don't start without me!" I yelled as I made my way over to Terri. I lifted my arms to match hers. "We're a chipmunk short. Where's Simon?"

"Around."

"We need to find her." I grabbed Terri's hand and took our interpretive dance on the road, roaming around trying to find Grace.

We discovered her in the corner of the room kissing Derrick Walker, who was dressed as Harry Potter.

I let out a gasp and threw my hand over my mouth. I hadn't meant to interrupt, but they heard me. Both of them looked in our direction.

"Don't mind us," I said, pulling Terri away. "Go back to kissing the Boy Who Lived."

"Wait," Grace called out. "Hey," she said, joining us.

"Why are you over here?" I asked her. "Go hang out with Derrick."

"That—that's nothing," she said.

Terri wiggled her eyebrows up and down. "It didn't look like nothing."

Grace chewed her lip. It was her tell. She was hiding something, something other than making out with Derrick at the party.

"What's going on?" I asked. "Whenever I mention Derrick, you get all weird. You've been doing it for weeks."

"It's just, it's just . . . nothing."

"Spill it," I said.

"All right." She looked so serious, but she still had the Simon glasses on. It made it hard to keep a straight face while looking at her.

"Come on, it can't be that bad," I said.

"Well . . . Promise you won't get mad?" she asked.

That was never a good start. I had no idea what I was in store for now. Any laughter I was feeling disappeared with her last words. "Just tell us."

"Okay." She squeezed her eyes shut. "Derrick and I are kind of serious. Pretty much since the beginning of the year. I was going to tell you," she said quickly, before either Terri or I could interrupt. "It was just . . . you were so upset about Marc, I didn't want to rub it in that I had a boyfriend. I thought I'd wait a little, and then you were really determined to find someone new, so I thought why not wait until you found him." She paused slightly and opened her eyes to peek at me. "And then you met Spence, and I was going to say something, but oh God. Okay, don't take this wrong. I didn't think he was good for you, and I was worried that if you thought I had a boyfriend, you'd stay in the relationship longer."

I felt numb. I just stared at her and the words kept tumbling from her mouth. "You were so set on having a boyfriend, and kept saying how not having one was the worst, so I thought it would be easier for you if I wasn't part of a couple, either."

I felt like she'd dropped a cement brick on my head. "You've had a boyfriend and didn't tell us?"

"I wanted to."

Terri looked like she was about to say something, but then stopped.

The crappy feeling that was overtaking my body multiplied. "You knew, too, didn't you?" I asked her.

"Don't blame her," Grace said before Terri could answer. "I begged her not to tell."

I pulled the hat off my head and clutched it tight. "So you told her and not me?"

"She figured it out."

"Great," I said, squeezing the hat. "Not only do you think you can't tell me things, but I can't even figure them out on my own."

Grace shook her head. "That's not it. I just wanted to make it easier for you."

"We're friends. Best friends. I want you guys to be happy. I don't want you hiding things from me. How could you think I wouldn't have wanted to hear about Derrick?"

She grabbed my hands. "I'm sorry. Terri told me to tell you. I just thought . . . I wasn't thinking."

"Do you think I'm that bad of a friend?" I was holding back tears. I couldn't believe she didn't tell me. "I would've been excited for you."

Grace squeezed her fingers around mine. "I know, and you're a great friend. I was trying to be one, too. I wanted to be there for you."

"It's true," Terri said. "She knew you'd ask questions and want to hear everything. She was afraid you would go home and think about what you were missing."

That feeling when Marc dumped me? This was a close second.

"I'm sorry," Grace said. "You have to forgive me. Please?"

I nodded.

Despite standing in a room full of people, I suddenly felt very alone. "I'm going to get some air," I said. Then I ran out of the party.

Chapter 34

I sat down on the steps outside Gretchen's house. I didn't feel like being at the party anymore, but I couldn't leave. Terri was my ride.

I pulled my jacket tighter around me.

"Cam?"

I thought it would be Grace or Terri, but it was Avery, coming to my rescue once again. Her cousin was with her. "I saw you run out here—are you okay?" she asked.

I shook my head. "But I will be."

"What can I do to help? Do you want to get out of here? Do you need a ride?"

I smiled at her. Despite being dressed as a cheerleader, she really was Wonder Woman. "You are not leaving this party for me. I'm just going to call my parents; they'll come get me."

"We can take you. Ty only had Diet Coke—he's totally fine to drive. Right?"

He nodded.

Now I was ruining Avery's night, too? I really was a sucky friend. "No, you've been talking about this party all week. You're not missing it."

"I could take you," Ty said. "I'm ready to go. You'd be doing me a favor. Avery, too. She's had to babysit me all night, and I'm pretty sure it's kept a few guys from coming over to talk to her."

I wasn't sure if he was just being nice or if he meant it.

"Come on." He held out his hand to help me up. "I was going to bail on this thing soon anyway."

I took his hand and stood. "How will you get home?" I asked Avery.

"Terri saw me come out here. She texted me. I just wrote her back. I told her my cousin was driving you home, and she said she'd take me and Nikki. Okay?"

"Yeah, thanks."

Ty turned to Avery. "If something happens or she's drinking, text me. I'll come get you."

Avery squeezed his arm. "Sometimes he goes into older cousin-slash-brother mode."

"Gotta look out for my biggest fan," he said, and gave Avery a hug goodbye. I did, too, and a few minutes later I was directing Ty to my house.

"You know," he said, "if you want to talk about it to someone who's not involved in the situation, or to take your mind off things, I have a few hours to kill. We could grab something to eat."

I swear Avery and her family were like my guardian angels, swooping in when I was at my lowest. "You don't have to do that."

"I know. It's for me, too. My other options are going back to a party and trailing around my cousin some more or sitting alone at Avery's house. Her parents and mine went to a movie."

"If you really want to do something," I said, "I do have one idea."

"Yeah?"

"We could watch *Mary Poppins*."

His face broke into a grin. "Sounds perfect."

"Cam?" my mom said when I opened the door. "You're home early." Her eyes widened and her hand went to the pore strip on her nose when she saw Ty. She had one on her forehead and another on her chin, too. "Oh, I didn't realize you had company. Hello."

I wanted to ask if that was what she'd worn to scare away trick-or-treaters who'd come to the door, but I didn't want to embarrass her more than I already had. I really should have given her a heads-up that I was bringing someone over. "Mom this is Ty, Avery's cousin. Is it okay if we watch *Mary Poppins*?"

"Sure." She looked like she had a million questions. Not that I blamed her. It must have seemed odd that I'd ditched a Halloween party with my friends to come home to watch a children's movie with a stranger. Whatever she was thinking, whether it was about Ty, me, or her pore strips, she didn't say anything. She just went back to her room, which I appreciated. It helped that Jemma was spending the night at a friend's, so I wasn't going to get the third degree from her, either.

I got us some drinks and popcorn and set the movie up.

"Cam?" Ty asked.

I'd spaced out for a minute. "Sorry, my mind is in a million places."

He looked at me, waiting for me to go on, and I did. Everything that had happened poured out of me. "I hate that they wouldn't tell me. We always tell each other things. Since forever."

"You go way back?" he asked.

I nodded. "Nine years ago, I really wanted to be in Girl Scouts, but the troop met Tuesdays after school, and I had Hebrew school. Everybody in my class was in the troop, except Grace. She had Korean lessons that day. We both felt left out.

"To cheer us up, Mrs. Kim and my mom decided that after our respective classes, we should all go out for ice cream. A few months later, Terri moved down the street from Grace. Mrs. Kim suggested she join us so she could get to know some kids in town. We wound up becoming best friends."

I grabbed a tissue and blew my nose. "I mean, what kind of person do they think I am? Don't they know I want them to be happy?"

"It sucks," he said. "But I do think they know that. I think they were worried about you and thought they were doing the right thing—that they were helping you."

Maybe he was right, but I still hated how they'd done it. Keeping things from me wasn't the way to help me. Marc had lied to me; I didn't need my friends to do it, too.

"Are you going to talk to them? It could help."

I wiped my nose. "Yeah, but I need a little time. I need to calm down." It hurt that they thought I worried more about my love life than I cared about them.

I turned on the movie, and for the next two-plus hours, I was able to get swept up in the world of *Mary Poppins*.

"Okay," Ty said when it ended. "You were right. That was great. Dick Van Dyke was brilliant."

"Told ya," I said, already feeling a little better. Some "Supercalifragilisticexpialidocious" would do that. "Have you heard the *Mary Poppins* theory?" I asked him.

"No." He leaned forward, his elbows on his knees, waiting for me to explain.

"They say she was Bert's nanny when he was a kid. It's why he knows all about her magic and the word *supercalifragilisticexpialidocious*. He even says something about learning it when he was 'just a lad.'"

He sat back. "Oh my God. That makes so much sense. I never would have thought of that. If anything, I thought there was a romance brewing between the two."

"Yeah, the writer of the Mary Poppins books actually wanted Disney to remove any traces of romance from the movie."

He lifted his hands to his temples and pulled them away as if his head were exploding. "This is going to make me take a whole new look at the character—it could change the entire dynamic. You just gave me a lot to think about."

"Well, you did the same for me. Thank you for listening to me vent about my friends."

"Of course."

I walked him to the door, and we said goodbye.

"Good luck with everything," Ty said. "And just so you know, from what I can tell, you are a good friend. Avery wouldn't hang out with anyone who wasn't."

"Thanks," I said.

I watched him get in the car, and then I went up to my room. I really hoped he was right.

Chapter 35

> **GRACE**
> You're not taking the bus.

> **TERRI**
> This is getting ridiculous, Cam.
> You need to talk to us.

Grace and Terri had messaged me a lot over the weekend, but I kept telling them I just needed time. They said they understood, but it seemed that understanding had run out now that it was Monday morning and we were due back in school.

It wasn't like I hadn't been thinking about them just because I wasn't talking to them. They were pretty much the only things on my mind. I kept playing what had happened over and over, trying to figure out how we'd gotten to a place where they felt they couldn't be honest with me. Between that and putting the finishing touches on the signs and program for Terri's art show, my brain was filled with a twenty-four-hour Grace-and-Terri news cycle all weekend.

I stared out the window of the school bus, watching the trees whip by, trying to figure out what to say before writing them back. I was at a loss, but I responded anyway.

> I know. I will. You said you understood and would give me some space.

TERRI
And we did. We didn't come over all weekend. But we need to hash this out. We'll be there in 15 to pick you up.

They were too late.

> Already on the bus. We'll talk after Terri's thing.

GRACE
That's not until tomorrow night!!!!!!!!!!!!!!

> Yeah, and I want that to be the focus. Not what's going on with us.

GRACE
. . .

TERRI
. . .

Whatever they were going to say, they changed their minds, and I was relieved. I wasn't ready for a real talk, and I meant what I'd said—I wanted the art show to take center stage, not our issues. Obviously, the hurt I felt over what happened hadn't gone away yet, but I still wanted to make sure everything went smoothly tomorrow night. It was important to me that Terri go to the school of her dreams. I wanted that for her, and I wanted to help make it a reality. For now, that meant not talking about what had happened between us. I was not risking one of us saying something we'd regret, or emotions getting out of hand. It was better to wait, to just put everything off until the show was over.

The bus pulled up to the school, and I trudged off with the rest of the students. If anyone thought it was unusual that I'd taken the bus, they didn't let on. They didn't even seem to notice me; it was like I was invisible. It was how I hoped to stay for the rest of the day.

I avoided my locker, afraid that my friends would be waiting for me, steered clear of hallways I knew they took, and waited until the last possible minute to get to any class that we shared. I felt Terri staring me down first period in statistics, but I was careful to never fully look in her direction.

It was like dodging Marc all over again, only worse. This was playing keep-away from my two very best friends.

They were waiting for me at the end of last period, hovering by Ms. Jackson's class. I accidentally looked straight at them. I couldn't pretend I hadn't seen them, so I gave a little wave and a meek smile.

"Catch you guys tomorrow night," I said, not stopping to chat.

If they tried to respond, I couldn't tell; the halls filled pretty quickly, and I let myself get caught in the shuffle toward the exit.

I felt empty. Not having Grace and Terri to talk to was a weird feeling. One more day. I could do this. The art show was almost here, and then we'd all talk, or fight, or whatever it took to figure things out.

I got back onto the bus. I'd taken it more today than I had all year.

"Cam?"

My head jerked at the sound of my name.

"Lissi?"

"Hi," she said.

I took the seat behind her. "Hi. I didn't know you were on this bus."

"Yeah, I take it when Ma—I mean, when I don't have a ride home."

I would have thought the idea of Marc giving her rides, something he'd always done for me, would have made me feel sad, but it didn't. I didn't feel anything. Not about that, anyway.

"I've never seen you on here," she continued.

"Terri and Grace usually have me covered on getting to and from school."

"Nice," she said, and then there was a long awkward pause as the bus started up. There was a lot of talking around us, but Lissi and I just sat there.

"I'm on Greenwillow Boulevard," she offered, breaking our silence.

Oh. She lived close by, super close by. "I'm two streets over, on Quietbrook."

Her eyebrows lifted.

"Yeah." I'm pretty sure my face matched her surprised expression. "Who knew? I guess this will make it easy to work on the yearbook."

She gave me a tentative smile. "You, um, mentioned getting together this week, right? Now that volleyball's over, my schedule is a lot emptier, so just let me know when."

I had told her that. I shrugged my shoulders. There was no time like the present. "If you're free today, you can come over whenever."

Lissi's nose scrunched ever so slightly as she considered my offer, and then she nodded. "Let's do it."

"Okay," I agreed.

Lissi and I had just made official plans to hang out.

What was going on? I was ignoring my best friends and hanging out with my one-time archnemesis? I might as well have been in an episode of *Stranger Things*, because I definitely felt like I was living in the Upside Down.

Chapter 36

issi and I planned to meet at my house after we both finished dinner, and right at seven thirty there was a knock on the front door.

My sister answered it.

"You've got to be kidding me! You're her, aren't you?" Jemma asked, blocking the entryway.

Oh no.

"What?" Lissi asked.

"I saw you on GroupIt. You're the one who stole Marc."

"Jemma!" I screamed, racing down the stairs. "Go." I pushed her out of the way, but that didn't keep her from staring Lissi down. This night was off to a great start.

Jemma peered out from behind me. "Why are you here? Do you really think Cam wants anything to do with you? Get a clue."

"Mom!" I screamed as I glowered at my sister. "Will you please get your daughter?"

"Jemma, come here," my mom called out.

My sister backed out of the room, but not without making a bigger spectacle. She took two fingers and pointed to her eyes and then turned them on Lissi, warning her that she was watching her.

Mortifying. There really wasn't any other word.

"I'm so sorry," I said to Lissi. "Please ignore my sister. I do."

I knew Jemma thought she was protecting me, but she'd just made an already awkward night even worse.

"I can go," Lissi said. She tugged a piece of her hair, circling it around her finger so tightly, I thought she was going to lose circulation.

I shook my head. "No, I want you here. I can use the help. I pulled up the pages you sent onto my computer," I told her, trying to pretend the incident with my sister hadn't happened. "Why don't we go take a look?"

Lissi followed me upstairs.

"Can I get you anything?" I asked, even though any attempt at being a gracious host would be overshadowed by what had happened at the front door. "Soda, water, snack?"

"No, I'm good," she said, not meeting my eyes.

Yeah, this wasn't weird at all.

"Have a seat, make yourself comfortable." I brought up an extra chair so that we could both sit at the computer.

I caught her looking at my wall of pictures. There were still a few with Marc in them, some group shots that I couldn't bring myself to destroy. When she realized I was watching her, she changed her focus to the computer.

"This shot is my favorite," she said, pointing to one of Avery mid-flip during the rally, "but the lighting is off."

"I can fix it," I said, opening Photoshop. A couple of clicks and the picture was perfect.

"Oh, wow, you're really good at that," she said.

"Thanks."

We swapped out a couple of images, fixed the color on some others, but we didn't talk much. When we had something to say, it was about the work, but even that conversation was stilted.

"Okay," Lissi said, after about ten minutes of pure tension. "Are we going to talk about it or what?"

"What do you mean?"

She gave me a look. I knew exactly what she was talking about—the elephant in the room.

"What's there to talk about?" I asked. We were getting along. Well enough to maintain a working relationship, anyway. Why rock the boat?

She shrugged. "I don't know. Why I wanted to work on the yearbook, or what happened with Marc? If the situation was reversed, I'd have some questions."

I had to press my hands into my legs to stop them from shaking. *Stupid nervous tic.* The truth was, there were things I wanted to know, but I didn't really want to get the information from Lissi. Would she be honest?

Questions swirled through my head. Marc had never answered what I'd asked him the night we broke up, and I *did* want to know some things. Curiosity got the best of me. I started with an easy ask. "Why did you agree to work on the yearbook?"

Lissi shrugged. "I like taking pictures and playing around with layout. I was supposed to be doing it at my old school, and I guess it felt like a way of getting my life back. Moving here at the start of senior year wasn't my choice. When I found out it was you in charge of the yearbook, I wasn't going to join. But then Ms. Jackson approached me about it again, and I don't know. I'd already given up so much moving here. I didn't want to miss out on something else. And if I'm honest, a little part of me was curious."

"Curious?"

"About you. You went out with Marc, Grace talked about you all the time—so did the others on the team. Even the soccer guys told stories about you. Good ones," she clarified.

I thought they had forgotten all about me. When Marc dumped me, it was like they did, too.

"When did you two meet?" I blurted out. "You and Marc." That was what I really wanted to know.

She took a deep breath. "Beginning of summer. I had gone into the school to talk about getting on the volleyball team and a few other things. I bumped into him when I left; he had finished soccer practice."

Part of me didn't want to hear the rest of this, but part of me had to know. "When did you two start dating? Did you know about me?"

Lissi sucked her bottom lip before continuing. "It wasn't right away. We just talked at first. I didn't know anyone else here, and he was someone to hang out with, but it grew into more. I didn't know about you. Not initially, but . . ." She looked away. "He kissed me, or started to, before he pulled away. He said he had a girlfriend, but that it was over, and that he was planning to end it, but wanted to do it in person. He said you were at camp, and that it wasn't fair to do it over the phone. He said he was going to do it when you got back."

Marc couldn't do it on the phone, but he could in the middle of a crowded diner? I had a pit in my stomach, and it was growing. "He didn't, though. We hung out when I got back, and the whole first week of school, he never said anything. Not one word about you or breaking up. He pretended everything was the way it always had been."

Lissi nodded. "I know. He was trying to find the right time. We fought about it. I told him it wasn't fair, to you or me, and that he had to tell you or I was done."

I didn't know what to say. How long would he have strung me . . . us . . . along?

"I'm really sorry," she said.

"You should be!" Jemma shouted.

I got up and opened my door. "Go!" I shouted back, and slammed the door shut again.

I shook my head. "I swear."

"It's nice," Lissi said. "She's trying to protect you."

At least Jemma had managed to break the tension—momentarily, anyway. I still had questions that needed answers.

I sat back down and looked Lissi straight in the eyes. "There were pictures of me and Marc all over the place. You never friended him on GroupIt or followed any of his pages?" I asked. "You would have seen us. Why would you want someone who cheated on his girlfriend?"

She swallowed. "I saw pictures of you, but I thought they were from the past or that you were just one of his BFFs. I guess I didn't really think about it . . . or didn't want to. When he said something, it was kind of too late. I liked him. A lot. And I didn't know you. It wasn't like we were friends. Plus, he told me that even if I hadn't been in the picture, he wanted to end things with you, and I believed him."

That one hurt. He would have ended things anyway? Was that true or was it just something he had told her? Either way, it sucked.

This isn't Lissi's fault, I reminded myself.

Still . . . I let out a long breath.

"I wish it didn't happen this way," she said.

That made two of us.

"And you know," she said, giving me a hopeful smile, "my aunt married my mom's ex-boyfriend and they all get along great, so it can happen. Maybe we can, too." She held up crossed fingers.

She was trying, I'd give her that.

"I guess you never know," I said. I wasn't on board with the idea, but I wasn't going to write it off, either. I wasn't sure what else to say, so Lissi and I got back to focusing on the yearbook.

It was still weird, but it felt more relaxed.

We worked steadily for two hours. We kept the conversation to the task at hand, and then Lissi's phone rang.

"Sorry," she said, fumbling to turn it off.

I recognized the ringtone. "Is that 'Alfie's Song (Not So Typical Love Song)'?"

She shrugged. "Yeah, I may be a little obsessed with *Love, Simon*."

"Oh my God. I love that movie. I'm the biggest rom-com fan you'll ever meet."

"Yeah?" She smiled. "Me too. I can't get enough. Movies, TV shows, books, you name it. I even got the romance package on Audible, and I try to squeeze it in whenever I can, including when I walk from one class to the next."

"That is such a good idea." I'd been wasting so much time not doing that.

For the next hour we wound up talking about our favorite books and movies.

When she left, I pulled up Lissi's GroupIt page. The anger and the resentment I'd felt for the past couple of months had evaporated.

My finger hovered over the friend-request icon.

I pushed it.

A couple of minutes later, a new notification popped up.

It said: You and Lissi Crandall are now friends.

I smiled. Sometimes life had ways of surprising you.

Chapter 37

On Tuesday, I made it through another school day without hanging out with Terri and Grace. We texted a little, but it was just making sure everything was good to go for the get-Terri's-parents-to-support-art-school plan. Grace said she'd dropped all the artwork at the restaurant last night (she raided the Marins' basement while Terri was on a date), and Terri confirmed (again) that she and her parents would be attending—even though they still had no idea exactly what they had RSVP'd to (Grace had remained pretty tight-lipped when Mr. Marin questioned why she needed the art—only giving away that it was part of the surprise). Other than that, we didn't communicate at all.

Despite everything, I was still excited for the show. Terri and the rest of the Marins weren't getting to the restaurant until six that night. Grace and Luke were getting there at five to help set up, but I got there at four. I figured I could get everything done before they arrived and avoid any awkwardness.

After I'd hung one last painting on the wall, I stood in the center of the room and admired the display.

I covered my mouth with my hand. The place looked amazing.

Terri was sooo talented. Her parents had to let her pursue her passion. She was too good to give up her dreams.

I checked the time. It was almost five. I ducked out of the restaurant and didn't come back until just before six.

"Cam!" Grace said when I walked back in.

"Hi."

She bit her lip. "Can we talk?"

"Yeah. After." I pointed outside. "I want to wait for the Marins. Escort them in."

Grace didn't object, but it looked like she wanted to. It killed me to keep being so short with her, but I had to be. I didn't want to break down; I needed to pull it together for Terri. Today was about her and her art, not me and my drama.

Terri and her family showed up right on time. I donned my biggest smile and brought them inside.

Luke and Grace were waiting by the entrance to the back room.

"What's this all about?" Mr. Marin asked.

"Welcome to Terri's first art show," I said.

Luke gestured for them to go in. We all followed.

Terri spun around, looking at all of us—and at all her pieces placed around the room. The expression on her face didn't disappoint. It was better than I'd imagined. It was astonishment, pride, confusion, and happiness, all rolled together. Her mouth opened as if she was going to say something, but no words came out. For once in her life, Terri didn't have anything to say. She was speechless.

I handed her and her parents a little booklet. The cover had one of her paintings, an intricate piece composed of thousands of dots that she'd made in art class. Underneath it was the date, location, and name of the event: *Terri Marin Art Show: An Exhibition of New Work.*

"You guys should walk around, take a look at everything," I told them.

We had picked a variety of pieces: watercolors, portraits, abstracts, and sculptures. Her family had seen most of them before, but not presented like this. *This* was striking.

"Cam," Terri said, stepping closer, but I didn't let her finish. "Go," I whispered. "Give your parents a tour. Really show them how important this is to you. *And* make them read the signs and look at the booklet."

She looked stunned, but then took them to the first piece. It was a realistic-looking sculpture of a woman's head. Next to each piece was a sign with careers you could end up with when you had skills like Terri's. For that particular sculpture's sign I'd written about the movie *Ant-Man*. Dating Spence had proved valuable in the end. After we'd watched *Ant-Man*, he'd shown me how they often used models to make the main character look big or small.

Terri said her parents' main argument for not wanting her to go to an art school was that they were afraid she wouldn't get a good job. They wanted her to have something to fall back on. So I'd decided to highlight work you could get because of the arts.

I'd included a lot of possibilities: website designer, graphic designer, cartoonist, animator, artistic director at an ad agency or publishing company, video-game designer. Making logos for brands, covers for books, and on and on.

In the booklet I also wrote about how Terri would learn new skills like 3-D rendering and 3-D printing and be ready to jump into new markets.

I included a story told by Jim Carrey, where he talked about how his father didn't follow his own dream of being a comedian. He went with the "safe job" and became an accountant. He got fired.

I thought the quote from Carrey was pretty powerful. He said, "I learned many great lessons from my father, not the least of which is that you can fail at what you don't want, so you might as well take a chance on doing what you love."

Then, on the very last page, I reminded them that if the liberal arts were that important to them, they should let her apply to RISD—that students there could cross-register for classes at Brown.

I hoped it would help Terri's case.

Her parents spent a good half hour walking around and taking everything in. We all watched them in silence, hoping they'd let their daughter follow her calling.

Mrs. Marin tapped the program. "We'll look at this in more detail when we get home. You certainly gave us a lot to consider."

"The evening's not over," Luke said. "If you'll follow me, I'll take you to your table for dinner, courtesy of the restaurant."

"Luke!" Terri said. "You don't have to do that."

"You're one of my best friends and this is your first gallery show. Yes, I do." He winked at her. "Consider it your birthday, Christmas, and graduation present."

"It's too much," she said. "We can't accept it."

"You better," Luke said, laughing. "I agreed to work New Year's Eve to make this happen—don't make it be for nothing. Paisley will destroy us both."

"Thank you," she said, and kissed him on his cheek. Then she turned to her parents. "Mom, Dad, can you go with Luke? I'll be there in a minute."

They followed him out.

Grace, Terri, and I were left in the gallery.

"You guys," Terri said, tears flowing down her face. "I don't know what to say."

"I'm taking it those are happy tears?" Grace asked.

"Yes." Terri's voice was quiet. "Why—how—when did you do this?" she stammered.

"Why?" I answered. "Because we love you, and we said we would help convince your parents."

She wiped her eyes. "I should have expected the queen of rom-com to pull off a grand gesture like this." Terri fanned herself with the booklet to quell her tears. It didn't work.

"My parents said they're amazed by how much you all care about me, but I'm not. I knew. I've always known."

Grace sniffled, tears rolling down her face, too. "Same here." She turned to me. "Cam, I never thought you were a bad friend. Please don't think that. I was just stupid. I thought I was making things easier for you."

Now I was crying, too. "But first Marc was keeping things from me, then you. I don't know . . . it made me feel like I wasn't enough and that you thought going after some guy meant more to me than you did."

She shook her head. "Never." She gave me a hug, and Terri wrapped her arms around us both. "I mean it."

"Me too," Terri said. "This not-talking has been killing me. I need my Cam updates."

"And I need you guys," I said. We were still standing there, arms wrapped around one another, crying. It was a good thing we were in a private room; we probably would have freaked out the rest of the restaurant.

I looked at Grace. "You know I want you to be happy, right? I'm excited for you and Derrick. I want to hear the details and all of that."

"I know, and you will. I'm sorry. Are we okay?" Grace asked.

"Yes," I said. "Just promise no more secrets."

"I promise," Grace said, letting go and wiping her eyes.

"Well . . . ," Terri said, stepping back. "If we're doing no more secrets, I guess we should let you in on one more thing."

My stomach rolled. "What?"

Terri jumped up and down.

My queasiness gave way to curiosity. The way she was acting, it definitely didn't seem like it would be a bad revelation.

"We have a surprise. We've been working with your parents to let us go on a girls' weekend to New York City over Thanksgiving weekend," she squealed. "We'll get to look at colleges for you, hang out, see the city."

I covered my face with my hands; the tears were coming faster now. "You didn't."

"We did," Grace said, squeezing my shoulder. "Guess you're not the only one who knows how to do a grand gesture."

Chapter 38

Marc walked out of the art room right as I passed by at the end of the day on Friday. I could feel his eyes on me.

"What?" I stopped and turned to him.

"Nothing."

Ever since the bonfire, I'd caught him looking at me all the time. At lunch, in the halls, even in the parking lot. "I've seen you more the past couple of weeks than I have the last two months. What gives? Why do you keep watching me?"

"I'm not." He rubbed his neck. Something was up. I peeked inside the art room. Ms. Winters and the rest of the class had already cleared out, so I pulled Marc inside.

"You are. What is it?" It felt strange being in a room with Marc, just him and me. It used to feel so natural; now it felt off.

"Look, Cam, I'm sorry."

Now he was apologizing? I didn't know what to say, so I didn't say anything.

He sat down on one of the stools. "I shouldn't have handled things like I did."

I thought I was finally over the breakup, over *him*, but the tears that stung at my eyes were telling another story.

"You cheated on me."

"No, it wasn't like that. I just wanted to break it off in person. I owed you that."

I sank onto the stool next to him and snorted. "Yeah, and that's why you didn't say anything when I got back from camp or the first days of school?"

He bit the inside of his cheek. "You were in such a good mood when you got back, and it was . . . I don't know. I didn't want to hurt you."

"Good job there."

Marc looked up at me. "I shouldn't have done it at the diner. I was scared; I thought it would be easier."

I worked to keep my voice even. "You were a coward."

He nodded. "I never meant for any of it to happen. I just met Lissi and she was so . . ." He stopped himself.

"So . . . what?"

"It doesn't matter."

"Tell me," I pressed. "I want to know."

"Fine." He massaged his neck. "She was different. Passionate about everything. Getting on the volleyball team, going to college back in New Hampshire, all the things she used to do at her old school."

"And you didn't think I was passionate? Did you not see me at your games? Or working my butt off to get into Columbia. Or how much I love my friends?"

Marc adjusted his back in the seat. "It wasn't the same."

"What are you talking about?"

"I mean, yeah, you were into all of that, but were you really? If I wasn't on the soccer team, would you have been interested in the games?" he asked.

"Who cares?" I countered. "I was supporting my boyfriend. That's a quality people like. I would have liked to have been supported."

"In what?"

"In anything."

"I supported you, but your interests were *my* interests. It felt like you didn't have anything of your own."

I felt adrenaline rush through my veins. "Maybe you didn't know me the way you thought you did. Maybe I didn't run across a field kicking a ball, but I read at least two books a week and watched more movies than I could count. Did you ask me about them? No. But it wasn't your thing, so I didn't bring it up all the time the way you did with soccer. And sorry if hanging out with my friends wasn't exciting enough for you, but to me, they're everything. Passionate? I go after what I want. I'm the one who brought up New York. I was the one who wanted to go there, and I'm the one who's making sure she does everything in her power to get there now."

"Okay, sorry," he said.

We both got quiet again. I was so angry, but I wasn't even sure it was at Marc. I hated that he was right, and that I was to blame, too. I *had* been a follower, little Miss Eager-to-Please. Things Marc wanted to do, *I* wanted to do. I let him choose everything, what parties we went to, where we ate, who we hung out with—and the list went on. I'd even become head "unofficial" cheerleader for his games. Sure, I still had Grace, Terri, and Luke, but only them. I had hung out with a million people in middle school, but once high school started, it was like Marc's friends were my go-to group.

"You felt this way the whole time we were together?" I asked, once I calmed down a bit.

He shook his head. "No. Definitely not in the beginning. And then I guess I didn't really think about it until I met Lissi. She called me out on stuff, made me try different things. I guess it was . . ." He let his words trail off, before he could say *different* again.

I had a feeling that wasn't the word he had intended, but I figured I probably didn't need to hear how exciting he'd found her.

I squeezed my wrist. "I hate how you handled things," I told him. "You screwed that up, but the rest?" I took a deep breath. "It wasn't all your fault. You didn't know me, because I didn't show you. I only gave you a taste. The past couple of months have been eye-opening," I confessed.

"I noticed."

I raised an eyebrow.

"Come on, don't pretend. You obviously noticed that I noticed. It's why we're in here now." He gave me a smile. It was one that used to give me goose bumps. "You're more out there. You got this . . . I don't know what it is . . . confidence or something. Being Brooksy, and those weird dances, you seem more open. More free. It's hard to look away."

"I guess I'm doing things for me, not for you." Or for Spence, or for any guy. I was doing what made *me* happy.

"I wanted you to do things for you. I didn't know you weren't. I like this you. I liked the old one, too, but this one—I'd like to get to know her better."

My mouth dropped open. Was he saying he wanted me back? He didn't come right out with it, but it sure sounded like he was alluding to it.

I put my hands up. "Marc . . ."

His mouth twisted up into a smile again, and he latched onto my eyes. His gaze was so intense.

This was what I'd been hoping to hear after he dumped me. I had dreamed about it.

But now?

Sure, having Marc look at me like I was the World Cup trophy tugged at my memories—and my heart—but I didn't want him anymore. He'd hurt me, but I'd gotten over it—over him. I'd moved on.

The realization made me smile.

"You should get going," I told him. "Lissi's probably waiting."

Then I got up and left the room without turning back.

I deserved way better than Marc.

I knew that now.

Chapter 39

"Get closer," I instructed Terri and Grace as I held my phone out for a selfie in front of Mamoun's, an amazing little falafel restaurant we stopped by near NYU. "I need to remember this place. It's amazing."

"You know there's a Mamoun's in Connecticut, too, right?" Terri asked.

"Just smile," I instructed her, and snapped the picture. "And yes, I know, but it's not the same. Here I'd be able to roll right out of bed, and voilà, I'd be here."

"You want to eat falafel right when you wake up?" Grace asked.

"Maybe," I said, not ready to rule anything out. "But if not, I could just stroll a few more feet and go to the fruit stand. Five bananas for a dollar. That's a great deal."

"I'm pretty sure your dining hall will have bananas," she assured me.

"Fine, yes, maybe, but that's not the point." I spun around. "There's just so many options. Look at everything around here."

We started walking, and I kept pointing stuff out. "There's Starbucks, but see, there's also tons of cute cafés, too. And shopping." I pointed to a guy in front of a table of sunglasses. "They're even selling stuff on the street." I picked up a pair of red heart-shaped glasses. "Jemma will love these. I have to get them."

"You're not going with the ones that say 'I love New York'?" Terri joked.

"No." I stood up straighter. "That would be touristy, and I'm not going to be a tourist; I'm going to be an NYU student." I crossed my fingers and held them up.

"Yeah?" Grace asked. "No more Miss Columbia."

I shook my head and paid the guy for the sunglasses. "Not anymore."

It turned out Columbia was Marc's dream school. NYU was mine.

We continued walking, passing through the park. "This is where I want to be," I said. We'd looked at Columbia earlier today, and it was nice, but it felt like a regular campus. Sure, there were things surrounding it, but Morningside Heights, the section of Manhattan the school was in, didn't have the buzz, the vibe, of the Village. "Can't you just feel the energy around here? It's like magic running through the air."

Grace laughed. "Magic, huh?"

"Yes, and there's so much going on. They even have pop-up performances like that poetry jam by the sculpture."

"You mean the *Alamo*—or, as it's more commonly called, the Astor Place Cube?" Terri corrected me.

I smiled. Of course she would know the name of the artwork. "Yes, I'm not even that into poetry, but I like that you can get it just by walking outside. I want to go here so badly."

"Hmm," Terri said, rubbing her chin. "Who might have said that to you ages ago?"

I swatted her arm. "Yes, go ahead, tell me you told me so. You said I'd love NYU, and I do. I just hope I get in."

"You will," Grace said. "You have straight As, killed the SATs, and you upped your extracurriculars with yearbook and Brooksy."

"Don't forget organizing an art show," Terri said.

I nodded. There was also Ms. Jackson's letter of recommendation. She let me take a look, and after reading it, I was kind of fangirling myself. And I felt really good about my essay. It was about how being a badger had helped me find myself, but it was a lot more nuanced than that. "I'm going to send my application in as soon as we get home. Maybe even back at the hotel tonight."

"First," Terri said, "we still have a lot of things to see."

"Right," I said. "Should we check out SVA next?" Our gallery had worked: Terri's parents said she could apply to some art schools (including the School of Visual Arts), and if she got accepted (which I was sure she would), they'd let her go.

She shook her head. "Tomorrow. We did enough campus browsing for today."

"We have the theater tonight," Grace said, "but we still have a bunch of time before that and dinner."

I clapped my hands. "Bookstores. There are so many in Manhattan. I want to see them all."

"Of course you do," Terri said. "Maybe we'll find something good for Luke." This was an all-girls trip, so he wasn't invited, but we wanted to make sure he knew we were thinking about him, so we'd planned to get him some souvenirs. I'd already picked him up an NYU T-shirt (and one for me).

"I can find something for Derrick there, too," Grace said.

"Great," I said, "but first a slice of pizza."

Terri looked at me like I'd developed a third nostril. "Pizza! We just had giant falafel sandwiches, and we're going to dinner in a couple of hours."

"It wasn't *that* big, and I'll still be able to eat. Come on, this is New York City pizza. I have to try it. I'll be super quick."

She nodded.

"Pizza it is, then," Grace said, and I let out a cheer as we headed to get my slice.

"I can't believe you finished that," Terri said as I dropped my napkin onto my paper plate. The slice had been gigantic, way bigger than Connecticut slices.

"It was exactly what I needed, and now I'm energized to go book shopping."

We got up, and I headed to the trash to throw out my stuff.

"Hey, two o'clock," Terri said, whispering behind me. "Cute guy totally checking you out."

I turned around to look, and my eyes opened in surprise. "*Ty?*"

"Cam! I thought that was you."

I turned to my friends. "Guys, this is Avery's cousin Ty." I turned back to Ty. "Ty, this is Terri and Grace."

They exchanged hellos, and he smiled at me, showing off that little dimple of his. Ty gave a very slight nod. After everything I'd told him about my friend issues the night of the Halloween party, he looked happy that we were all standing there together.

"What are you doing here?" he asked.

"Checking out schools. What about you?" I asked.

"I go to NYU."

Of course he did. Terri jabbed me in the side, but I refused to look at her; I knew she'd make wiggly eyebrows or something at me.

"It's my first choice," I said.

"Well, if you have any questions, just hit me up."

"Thanks, I may take you up on that. It was really nice seeing you, Ty," I said, and gestured to my friends, "but we better get going."

"Have a great rest of your trip," he said.

"Whoa." Terri fanned herself when we got outside and out of Ty's earshot. "Why didn't you tell me how much hotter Avery's cousin is in person?"

"Yeah," Grace said to me, "do I smell a romance brewing?"

"Right now I think you just smell the sewers."

"Come on, you know what I'm talking about," she pressed.

"I guess we'll just have to wait and see."

I was open to possibilities, and if Ty was any indication of the type of people I'd meet over the next four years, I could tell it was going to be quite the ride. But right now, I wasn't thinking about guys.

"I can't believe I may actually get to live in this city. It's everything I want," I said. "Well, except for one thing."

"What?" Grace asked. "What could it possibly be missing?"

I squeezed my wrist. "You two. I can't believe we won't be going to school together. I'm going to miss you guys so much."

"Hey, don't get weepy on me now," Grace said, putting her arm around me. "We're having too much fun. Do you want me to start crying, too? It's only November. We have the whole rest of the year and the summer."

"I know."

"Besides," Terri said, attaching herself to my other side, "you can't get rid of us. If you ignore my texts and FaceTimes I'll just track you down."

I was pretty sure she wasn't joking.

"And how can you forget?" Grace asked, bumping her hip into mine. "True love always finds its way. Isn't that what you've been jamming down our throats with all those movies since the third grade?"

I nodded.

"Well," she continued, "isn't what we have real?"

"It is."

"Then that's that," Terri said. "You're going to be stuck with us for life."

I liked the sound of that.

I squeezed them closer to me. As it turned out, not all rom-coms needed to end with getting the guy, or the girl, or that fairy-tale magical kiss. They just needed to end with love, and I had that—in excess.

Acknowledgments

With each book I become more and more in awe of all the talented people at Swoon Reads and Macmillan. From the editorial team, the production editors and copy editors, the designers, the assistants, and the interns to the subrights, sales, marketing, publicity, digital, and advertising teams—you are all amazing. Thank you for all your help.

Jonathan Yaged and Jean Feiwel, thank you for helping make one of my dreams come true. I'm truly grateful for the opportunity you've given me.

Holly West—you believed in this book from the beginning, and it's so much better because of you. I'm so glad that I get to work with you. You are a dream editor.

Erin Siu, your notes and feedback were incredible and very much appreciated.

Lauren Scobell, you've been there with me through this whole journey, and I can't thank you enough for all that you do.

Liz Dresner and Karina Grande, I'm swooning over your cover! Thank you Morgan Rath for being a fantastic publicist; Kat Brzozowksi, Teresa Ferraiolo, and Emily Settle for all your social media posts; copy editor Karen Sherman and production editor Lindsay Wagner for making sure everything is up to par (and catching my mistakes!); Holly Ingraham for your feedback; Kristin Dulaney, Allison Verost, Melissa Zar, and everyone who's helped me along the way—thank you, thank you, thank you!

To my agent, Laura Dail, I'm still in awe that I get to be represented by you. I feel so fortunate to have you in my corner. Thank you—and your team—for everything. And a special shout-out to Samantha Fabien and Clare Curry for your amazing notes on this book!

To my fellow Swoon authors—the Swoon Squad—getting to know each of you has been so much fun!

To the booksellers, librarians, bloggers, and readers, your support does not go unnoticed. I'm so thankful for you.

To everyone at Fox 5, I feel like I've grown up at the station, and you've all become like a second family to me.

To my actual family (immediate and extended)—there are no words to express how much you mean to me. Please know I love you all.

Mom, Jordan, Andrea, Liam, and Alice—my wish is that you see yourselves how I see you—truly stunning inside and out and extremely loved.

To my dad, I miss you so much, but I know how proud you'd be of me and our whole family and how much you loved us. The feeling is mutual.

This book is about friendship, and I've truly been blessed with a wonderful bunch of friends. Thank you for being there for me through the good and the bad—and helping me smile through it all. (You may have even inspired moments in this book, like dramatic readings at poetry slams, truth-or-dare in a diner, supporting harebrained ideas that seemed really clever at the time, and showing what it means to be a friend.)

Some shout-outs: Cecilia, Christina, Michelle, Lauren, Adi, Jessica, Sandy, Susannie, Cara, Karen, Barry, Robyn, Lisa, Nadine, Keren, Phil, Holly, Erika, the family who are also friends, the new friends, the old friends, and the ones I may have accidentally left out (but will forgive me because that's what friends do ☺).

And to Ben Levkov, it took me a really, really long time to find you, but you were so worth the wait. There's no finding Mr. Better-Than-You, because you are my Mr. Better-Than-All-of-Them, my Mr. Right. You are truly incredible, and every day I think how lucky I am to have you as my partner. I love you.

Check out more books
chosen for publication
by readers like you.